FLYING MISS LOMAX

A SAPPHIC AGE GAP ROMANCE IN THE 1940S

AVEN BLAIR

CHAPTER 1

LAURA

Savannah Georgia March of 1949

As my photography crew and I wait to board Erin's impressive plane, now taxiing toward us, a smile tugs at my lips. I can't help but reminisce about how captivating she was years ago. Erin has always been my favorite fashion model to photograph. Even after 27 years behind the camera, she still holds a very special place in my heart.

Seeing her step out of the pilot's door instantly overwhelms me, rekindling memories of the emotional intimacy we once shared. As Erin walks toward me, anxiety and excitement flood my senses. She's now a confident, radiant woman. The years have changed her, but that same familiar spark remains, stirring up tender emotions I've spent the last eleven years trying to bury.

As Erin approaches, my heart knots with pain as I notice a long, pronounced scar on her left cheek, running down to her jaw. She is still beautiful, but she now bears a scar I feel compelled to understand. Glancing away from it, I meet her familiar earthy-green eyes—calming and serene—the very eyes I fell in love with all those years ago.

She walks into my arms, and I whisper her name, "Erin."

As she pulls me close, I feel both her strength and tenderness. Holding her, I realize just how much she's matured. She's no longer the nineteen-year-old I once captured so intimately through the viewfinder of my camera.

Erin was the only model with whom I ever felt such a deep connection through my viewfinder and in my life. There was something about the way she looked into the camera—and at me—that laid bare her raw vulnerability with just a subtle hint of attitude.

Releasing me, she pulls away and flashes a huge grin. "Hi, Laura. It's so good to see you again after all these years. I've missed you," she says warmly.

Smiling into her eyes, I carefully avoid letting my gaze linger on the scar, and reply, "You're so beautiful, Erin. You've grown into such a lovely woman. I've missed you too."

Enjoying our intimate reunion, I gaze once more into her calming eyes, before turning away to introduce her to my photography crew. "Erin, this is Julie Evans and Mark Sterling, part of Lomax Inc. And guys, this is Erin Winslow, our pilot and owner of *Blue Sky Aviation*. She'll be flying us to Maine and staying with us for the next few days.

"Let me get this straight," Mark says, placing a hand on his hip, his eyes lighting up with heightened enthusiasm. "So, you're a pilot, Erin, and this is your big ol' plane, honey?" he adds with his usual flamboyant flair,

"Yes, I am indeed a pilot, and this is my plane. Most of it belongs to the bank, but they're kind enough to let me keep her as long as I make the payments on time."

As we all chuckle, Mark throws his hands up dramatically and exclaims, "Oh hell, get away from me, girl!" We burst into laughter at his remark.

"Laura says you used to be a model, Erin," Mark says, resting his fist against his chin. "I can see that, honey—you're drop-dead gorgeous!" He then turns to me with a grin and adds, "Now I see why you talk about her so much."

Suddenly, I want the earth to open up and swallow me. I never know what will pop out of Mark's mouth, and this time he's completely embarrassed me. Erin gives me that vulnerable grin I've always adored, then winks at me.

"Let me deploy the boarding steps for you all," she says, walking away from me toward the plane. Julie and Mark are hot on her heels, eager to board. I hang back, waiting for them to load, hoping for a moment alone with Erin.

After Julie and Mark board with their luggage and all of our camera gear, Erin walks back to me, smiling. "I was surprised to hear from you a few weeks ago, but thank you for calling. I appreciate you hiring me, but I'm even more excited to see you, Laura."

"Well, the crew and I have flown commercial airliners over the past few years, but flying to the Maine location wasn't feasible. Besides, this gave me an opportunity—and a reason—to reach out to you again."

Erin gazes at me curiously and asks, "Why would you need a reason, Laura?"

Glancing away from her toward the plane, I realize what I've said. "I'm sorry, Erin. I just meant..."

"Laura, it's okay, forgive me. I never wanted to lose touch with you, but I understand why it happened. It doesn't matter now because here you are again, and you're even more beautiful than you were back then."

"Thank you, Erin, but I'm well aware that I've aged. However, you are indeed gorgeous, just as Mark said."

Smiling, she grabs my suitcase and says, "Come on, let's get you boarded." As we walk toward the boarding steps, she pauses. "There's plenty of seating inside, but

I'd love it if you sat up front with me for part of the flight."

"I'd love that, Erin. It will give us some time to catch up," I say softly, gazing into her earthy-green eyes again.

"Good, I'll look forward to it," she replies softly.

As I step into the plane, I notice that Mark has taken over the small sofa, stretching out comfortably. "Do you plan to commandeer that sofa for the whole trip?" I ask, settling into one of the club chairs across from Julie.

"Yeah, Mark, I got news for you: that ain't happening," Julie says firmly.

"We'll see about that, Miss Julie. I only have to move if Laura says so," he asserts rudely, reclining further and putting his hand behind his head.

Shaking my head, I laugh at the two of them. "We haven't even taken off, and you two are already bickering like old ladies."

After Erin closes the hatch, I hear her open the pilot door. I catch a glimpse of her in the pilot seat at the controls, grinning as I watch her. I can hardly believe the young model from so many years ago is now flying planes.

Mark and Julie continue their playful banter filled with humorous excitement. Despite their jabs and bickering, they've grown extremely close, after working with me for the past three years.

Both are in their late twenties, still young and playful at times—and often completely immature. However, when it's time to shoot, all of that falls away, and they become entirely professional, always anticipating my needs and the vision I have for the set. The three of us operate like a well-oiled machine, seamlessly coordinating every detail of the shoot with precision and ease."

As the plane ascends, I feel a rush of rejuvenation for my craft. Over the past few years, my photography has become familiar and repetitive, but something about this ascent has lifted my spirit. I'm not sure if it's seeing Erin again or if we're flying in a small, cozy plane instead of an airliner; either way, I plan to channel this excitement over the coming days. I'll definitely need it for this shoot.

Victor Voss is a demanding women's clothing brand I've worked with exclusively for their fall and winter line for the past five years. One aspect I enjoy about working with them is that I can focus solely on shooting, as they handle all the makeup and hair.

I often have to manage and facilitate these details myself with smaller brands. However, they are generally more flexible and less demanding than a large brand like Victor Voss.

We're well into the first hour of the flight, and Mark and Julie have stopped bickering at my request. Gazing out the window as I sit in the club chair, I enjoy the scenery and the hum of the plane. Looking back at Erin, I begin to do the math. She was only 17 when she started modeling and 19 when she stopped. That was eleven years ago, which makes her 30 now.

Grinning as I look back out the window, I wonder where the time has gone and how she could already be 30. But she is, and here she is, in the cockpit flying this beast. I can't stop grinning, both outwardly and inwardly. Why, I'm not exactly sure.

Erin invited me to sit with her, but each time I think of getting up to join her, I can't seem to move. She was too young back then, but as I gaze at her now, I wonder. Closing my eyes, I revisit the past and our closeness.

Erin was at my home almost every evening, whether we had a photo shoot or not. Our closeness grew intimate, and then one evening, as she helped me in my dark room, it happened—she kissed me.

The amber darkroom lights illuminated the room, casting

a warm glow and a spell over us. Before I had time to think, Erin was in my arms, and I was loving her. Her tender lips touched mine, and I wanted her so badly in that moment— but I had to pull away.

Opening my eyes, I feel a burning in them as that moment haunts me, filled with thoughts of what might have been. Erin was only 19, so I know I made the right decision, but it hurt me deeply. We tried to talk about it, but it was impossible to remain as close as we had been, simply intimate friends.

All these years, I've had to live with the knowledge that, in that tender moment bathed in the warm amber glow of the darkroom light, I both loved and lost her in that intimate, loving kiss. The pain is still there, and as I gaze at her, I begin to wonder if I should have chosen a different pilot.

After a few moments, the pain subsides, and I rise to join Erin. As I approach, she looks over her shoulder and gives me that smile I've seen through my viewfinder hundreds of times. "Is this seat taken?" I ask with a nervous chuckle.

"Well, this seat is reserved for someone very special to me," she says loudly so I can hear her over the noise from the engine and propellers. She then hands me a headset. As I sit next to her, I put it on, and Erin reaches over with a smile to adjust it. As our eyes lock, I hear her say through the headset, "I'm glad you joined me."

"Thank you for the invitation. Wow, it's a bit scary up here," I say nervously into the microphone of my headset.

Erin takes my hand and says, "You'll get used to it. Just give it a few minutes." Then she releases my hand. Suddenly, it's not my fear of heights I'm scared of. Her touch brought everything back, and now I'm gripped with fear. I stay silent as I look outward to hide my feelings. But as I gaze at the vast expanse below and the absence of solid ground beneath me, my anxiety and fear only deepen.

CHAPTER 1

After a moment, Erin asks, "Are you okay, Laura?"

I nod and remain silent.

"Laura, look at me, please." I turn toward her as she reaches for my hand again. "It's okay, I know." Smiling, I gaze at her, searching for the young woman who once broke down walls I had built years ago simply by being herself.

Our fingers intertwine as she holds my hand, and I feel the strength of the woman she's become. I'm overcome with an immediate longing. "Perhaps this wasn't a good idea, Erin," I say softly through my microphone.

She looks at me and grins. "I disagree; I think it's a very good idea," she says in a reassuring voice that suddenly soothes me. Smiling back into her calming eyes, I nod and grip her hand a bit tighter. She glances at our hands and then back at me. My heart falls, but I hold her gaze, feeling the uneasiness but also the magic that still lingers between us.

CHAPTER 2

ERIN

Holding Laura's hand feels familiar and soothing. Gazing out into the vastness, I continue holding her hand, I keep our fingers intertwined. I can't believe she contacted me to fly her and her crew to Maine, but it makes me incredibly happy. Since her call, I haven't been able to think of much else. The anticipation of seeing her again after all this time has been overwhelming.

She brought me so much comfort during the two years we grew close while I was modeling. I remember those evenings at her home, listening to *The Shadow*, *The Thin Man*, and *Jack Benny* on the radio, curled up on the sofa next to her warmth with popcorn and laughter.

"Do you ever listen to any of our old radio shows?" I ask, smiling into her warm brown eyes—the same eyes my nineteen-year-old self fell in love with.

Laura chuckles as she gazes at me, but then her expression turns solemn. Shaking her head, she says, "No, I couldn't listen to those anymore after you stopped coming over."

"Neither could I," I say, staring straight ahead.

"Maybe I should join the others."

"Please, Laura, I want you up here beside me."

Laura gives me her tender smile, the one that always makes me feel like I am the center of her universe. She nods, "Okay, but this is a bit harder than I thought it would be, Erin."

"Yes, it is," I say, looking at her, then add, "I'm not sure if you've noticed, but I'm not nineteen anymore, Laura."

Nervously, she says, "Oh, Erin, I've definitely noticed." Then she holds my gaze with a tender softness I've never felt from any other woman. I smile, letting her see the love I still hold for her. Then she adds, "How could I possibly not notice what a mature and vibrant woman you've become?"

"Thank you," I whisper through the headset as I look at her. "Laura, you genuinely are even more beautiful than you were eleven years ago," I say with conviction, holding her gaze.

She chuckles and glances out her side window, perhaps a bit uneasy from my compliment. Laura has never truly understood how beautiful she is. I've always felt she was on the wrong side of the camera. While she's an excellent photographer, she could have easily been a model herself.

It's been incredible having Laura remain in the cockpit with me over the past hour. She let go of my hand a while back, but having her this close again is just as nice. "I'll need to make a refueling stop soon. We'll be landing in Richmond in about an hour."

"Okay, those two back there could probably use a bathroom break. I'm just thankful they aren't bickering." she says with a laugh.

"They seem great, and I can tell they adore you," I say.

"Well, I often feel like Aunt Laura to them, but they're the best crew I've had. You wouldn't know it from how they bicker and fight, but they become completely different when it's time to shoot."

"I suppose they are well aware of your no-nonsense approach on set, Laura."

She gazes at me and asks, "Is that how you remember me?"

"Very much so, and I admired that about you."

"Thank you, Erin. I do take it seriously. I always have."

"And that's why you're the best fashion photographer out there," I say earnestly. Then I ask, "Laura, why haven't you moved to New York? Many of your assignments were always there."

She smiles sweetly at me and says, "Savannah is my home, Erin. I'll never leave her."

"Yeah, I feel the same way."

I glance at Laura and notice her serious gaze fixed on me. Then she asks, "Erin, what happened to you? I saw the scar on your face."

Looking out the windshield, my mind shifts to that moment of recklessness driven by my grief. "It happened about nine years ago. I had only had my pilot's license for about a year. One morning, I woke up distraught and depressed. I got into my beat-up plane that I should have never been flying. Anyway, the fog rolled in, and I lost my bearings. My plane hit the treetops near Tybee Island, then the marshland. Then it tumbled and broke apart."

As I pause briefly, I notice that, at some point during my explanation, Laura has taken my hand and is now holding it gently between hers. "Erin," she whispers through the headset. Laura's soft voice still moves through me like the first warm day of spring.

With warm chills from her tenderness, I continue. "As the plane broke apart and scattered across the marshland, so did

I. When I woke, it was late in the evening, with the sun setting. I tried to get up but couldn't. So, I lay there in a broken heap all night long, in pain, begging God to save me."

"My God, Erin, that had to be awful. It makes me hurt for you," Laura says tenderly.

Swallowing a lump in my throat, I reply, "It was. I drifted in and out of consciousness all night, but each time I woke, the sound of waves hitting the beach in the distance brought me a sense of calm."

"You always loved the beach, Erin. I'm glad the sound comforted you," she says, smiling while holding my hand.

Gazing back at Laura, I say, "The following day, I woke and somehow managed to sit up. I was bloody and battered, trying to stand but unable to. I knew my face was a mess, but I had no idea how bad it was.

It seems silly now, but as I sat there, broken, all I could think about was my face." I look out the windshield and add, "I remembered how much you loved my 'beautiful face,' as you used to say, and it made me sick to think it was probably completely damaged."

"Erin, honey. It was never about your beautiful face," She says as she glances back at Mark and Julie, who are sound asleep. Then she whispers through the headset, "I loved everything about you, Erin. When I gazed at you through my viewfinder, I didn't see just your pretty face," she adds, tenderly threading her fingers through my hair. "I saw your raw vulnerability, the side of you that you only showed me. I could see your kind and loving soul, Erin."

Closing my eyes briefly, I savor Laura's touch once again. God, how I've missed this woman; she has no idea how broken I felt after losing her. "Who found you, Erin?" she asks, her fingers gently threading through my hair.

"Well, later in the day, I realized that if I was going to

survive, I had to save myself. So, I crawled on my elbows and belly toward the sound of the ocean until nightfall, then lost consciousness again to the sound of the sea. My next memory was waking up in the hospital, surrounded by medical staff."

"What other injuries did you suffer?" she asks tenderly.

Looking into Laura's loving eyes, I continue. "I broke both legs in different places and had numerous lacerations across my body." Chuckling, I add, "If you think this scar is bad, you should see the one that runs the entire length of my back."

Laura's loving hands continue to comfort me as I recount that painful and traumatic time. Not wanting to share my internal scars, I simply say, "I'm just lucky to be alive and flying again."

"Yes, you are. And I'm not surprised you're flying again after that horrific incident. You've always been very strong-willed," she says with a smile.

"I suppose so," I reply with a grin. After checking the fuel gauge, I say, "Laura, I plan to land at Richmond Airport to refuel. We are about 400 miles into the flight so we'll need to make a quick stop to top off the tanks before continuing."

"Okay, should I move to the back?"

Smiling, I ask, "Don't you want to land with me? It might be a bit scary, but it's also a rush if you just relax and trust me."

"Oh, I trust you, Erin. Myself, not so much, but I'm enjoying being up here with you, so I'll just ride it out with you," she says as she repositions her body in the seat. Laura is clearly nervous about the descent, but I'm glad she's chosen to stay with me.

After contacting the Richmond tower, I begin descending the Beechcraft. As we land, I glance at Laura and notice her eyes are closed. Chuckling, I say, "We're on the ground now, Laura."

Laughing, she says, "That was a bit scary, but not as bad as I anticipated."

As I taxi toward the refueling tanker, I glance at her briefly to see if she is okay. In this brief moment, all I see is the beautiful woman I fell in love with so long ago.

CHAPTER 3

LAURA

After landing in Richmond to refuel, Julie and Mark immediately head for the restrooms and snack bar while I stay close to Erin. "Well, you and I might as well take a break, too; it will take them 20-30 minutes to refuel her," Erin says.

"That makes sense. I would imagine refueling the plane takes a while."

Before rising, Erin takes my hands and says, "Laura, this time with you has been wonderful. Thank you for inviting me back into your life."

Gazing at our hands, I smile and muster the courage to say, "I could have hired other pilots, Erin." I pause, then clear my throat and continue, "But I wanted to see you again. I want you back in my life, so there's no need to thank me."

As I gaze into Erin's earthy-green eyes, softened with maturity, I see more than friendship reflecting back. I'm sure my own desire to be more than friends is mirrored in her lovely gaze. I hope so because expressing it out loud feels far more difficult than allowing her to see it in my eyes.

We're back in the air, and I'm still in the cockpit beside Erin. "Thank you for remaining up here with me, Laura. I'm enjoying our time together."

I give her a warm smile. "So am I, Erin. I've truly missed you. We were almost inseparable back then; you were always a joy to be around."

"So were you, Laura. I loved spending time with you at your home. It was much calmer and less chaotic than my house, and I enjoyed being with you."

"Well, I loved you being at the house with me." Swallowing hard, I bravely say, "My home was very empty after you stopped coming over. It was extremely difficult without you in my life."

Erin remains silent, so I gaze at her and see her eyes glistening. Reaching for her hand again, I hold it tenderly, knowing how painful it must have been for her.

"We should have tried harder to remain close, Laura. At the time, it seemed impossible, but we should have tried. I regret that."

Laura interlaces her fingers with mine. "Yes, we should have, Erin. I'm glad you've agreed to become part of my life again."

"So am I," she replies, then gives me a sweet smile. I continue holding her hand, not wanting to release it as we continue our flight to Maine.

After a few moments, Erin suddenly bursts into laughter. "Remember that day we had just started a photo shoot at that large mansion outdoors by the pool?"

"Yes!" I exclaim as I join her in laughter. "I had all of you positioned exactly how I wanted, including those two girls whose names have escaped me."

Erin chimes in, "Claire and Joanna. They hated each other."

"Yes, they did. But I had no idea just how much until that day. What started it all?"

Erin laughs, "I think Joanna had been flirting with Claire's boyfriend, and Claire had just had enough. That was the last straw when Joanna stepped in front of Claire after you'd positioned everyone perfectly. Claire pushed Joanna backward toward the pool. As I reached out, trying to grab her, all six of us tangled together and ended up falling backward into the pool.

"Oh, Erin, stop! I'm dying. I can still see the huge splash when you all hit the water. It was like a bomb landed in the pool," I say, laughing.

Erin continues, "Then Claire and Joanna started fighting in the pool. At that point, I didn't care anymore; I just let them fight."

I was so frustrated, I remember helping you out of the pool, but I let the others sort themselves out. Then I packed my gear and called it a day."

"You never allowed those two on your photo shoots ever again," Erin says, continuing to laugh.

"No, I did not. That was completely unprofessional but very comical now as we look back at it. I grabbed you, and we went to my house and cooked dinner. That day was completely ruined."

"That seems like so long ago, but then again, it feels like only yesterday sitting next to you, Erin." I shake my head and ask, "Whatever happened to those two?"

Erin laughs again, saying, "Joanna married Claire's boyfriend about a year later."

"Seriously? Oh, poor Claire," I say sympathetically.

"There's no need to feel sorry for Claire; she married a wealthy guy from Atlanta, and now she has her own huge mansion—with a pool," Erin says, laughing.

"Well, that turned out okay for Claire then."

"Yeah, but not Joanna." Glancing at her with a quizzical look, Erin continues. "Joanna now lives with Claire's old boyfriend in the basement of his mother's home."

We both laugh hysterically. "Erin, you have to be making this up."

"No, it's the honest truth. I guess we really should be saying, 'Poor Joanna.'"

Our laughter grows louder as we fall back in sync, speaking in unison, 'Poor Joanna,' in a comically sad tone. Our laughter escalates, eventually waking Julie and Mark.

"What's so funny up there?" I hear Julie ask.

"Just a funny story from the past, Julie," I tell her as we continue laughing. As our laughter continues, Mark suddenly appears, sticking his head into the cockpit, so I gently release Erin's hand.

"You two have been talking and cackling for the past hour while I'm stuck back there with *"Betty Boop.""*

"Oh shut up, Mark, and leave them alone," Julie barks.

Looking at Mark over my shoulder, I say, "Go back to your sofa, *'Li'l Abner'* and leave us alone. We'll be in Camden in about two hours."

Julie shouts, *'Li'l Abner!?'* That's hysterical, Laura." Then she adds, "Mark, that's your new nickname the whole time we are in Maine. Come on *'Li'l Abner'* and sit back here with sexy *"Betty Boop,"* Julie says as she laughs loudly.

Mark rolls his eyes, straightens up, places his hands on his hips, and says, "Laura, you must really love Erin, honey, because I know you—and there is no one else on this planet who could get you to sit in the cockpit of a plane and look out at that scary mess."

I give him one of my famous glares—the kind he knows all too well. His eyes widen as he backs up slowly, hands raised in surrender. "Just going back to my seat now, so sorry," he mutters, then winks at me.

I take a deep breath, and when I look over at Erin, she's watching me with that soft, warm gaze that makes my heart skip. I give her a shy smile and shake my head, and she responds with a grin and a cute wink. All I can do is smile back, glance out my window, and savor how perfect this moment feels.

After a few moments, I reach for Erin. She takes my hand once again, our fingers intertwining. Every nerve in my body ignites with an aching, uncontrollable yearning as I feel the strength of her hand in mine. Then I replay in my mind those earthy-green eyes of hers on me and then her tender wink that quickly followed.

"Your hand feels different," I whisper to her into my headset's microphone.

She smiles and says, "That's funny because yours feels exactly how I remember it." Looking over the beautiful Atlantic Ocean, I gently press her hand, signaling that I am enjoying her presence. She responds with a soft, reassuring squeeze. I close my eyes and smile.

~

Camden Maine

It's mid-afternoon, and we have just landed at a small airport in Camden. "Well, that landing was much like the other one, except this time, I kept my eyes open," I say with a chuckle.

"Yes, you did, I'm proud of you. You looked completely relaxed this time, Laura. I might let you fly her home," Erin says in jest.

Laughing, I say, "Well, I'd like to actually make it home to Savannah, so I better leave that to you."

After Erin deploys the boarding steps, Julie, Mark, and I gather our luggage and multiple photo cases and disembark the plane. I watch Erin walk back up the steps and then close them. After a moment, I glance toward the plane and see Erin exiting from the pilot door. The breeze catches her short brown hair, and my heart tumbles as she gazes at me, smiling.

Approaching me, she says, "I'll need to stay behind and tie down the plane. Y'allYou go ahead, and I will catch up with you soon."

"I don't mind waiting with you, Erin."

"No, go ahead; I'll be there shortly," she replies. Then she leans toward me and whispers, "Will you have dinner with me tonight?"

Looking into her eyes, my heart aches and gently falls. I glance at Mark and Julie, who are loading our cases and luggage into the taxi, and then I look back at Erin. Moving close to her, I gently grip her fingers, look into her earthy-green eyes, and say, "Yes, most definitely." Erin gives me a wide smile.

Before I join the others in the taxi, I softly say, "I'll secure you a room close to mine, so when you get to *The Lexington Inn,* your room will be waiting for you." I say as our fingers intertwine once again.

As I gaze at Erin's face, I catch a glimpse of the nineteen-year-old model I fell in love with years ago. She offers me a shy smile, revealing the vulnerability she used to share only with me. "Thank you, Laura. I'll see you soon," she says, then gives me a sweet kiss on my cheek.

As I join the others in the taxi, I gaze out my window and see her already working with her plane; it makes me smile. Mark interrupts my tender thoughts of Erin. "Laura, it's cold as a witches titty up here. I'm not sure if this flawless skin of mine can take this frigidness."

Julie and I laugh at him. "Mark, I hate to break it to you, honey, but you are far from flawless, my dear," Julie replies.

I smile at the two of them as they continue their banter. My thoughts drift elsewhere. Lost in thought, I finally hear, "Laura...Laura?'

"Humm?" I say, unaware of who said my name.

"Laura, anyone home?" Julie says.

Smiling, I say, "Yes?"

Leaning toward me, Julie whispers, "Just exactly how close were you and Erin back then?" She asks. She grins at me and waits for my answer.

"Just close," I reply with a smile.

"Uh huh," Mark says, obviously overhearing Julie's question. Then adds, "That girl has it bad for you, Laura."

"Oh, Mark, hush," I quip.

Julie leans in toward me and whispers in my ear, "She's fucking adorable, Laura. I might have to fight you for her, and I'm not even *'that way.'*"

"Oh, Julie. She's someone very dear to me that I was close with years ago."

"Save it, Laura. I see how you look at her. Hell, honey, I've never seen you like this," Julie replies. Then adds, "I like this side of you, Laura. You know, not all serious and business-like."

"Can we please change the subject?" I say out loud so Mark can hear me as well.

"Yes, Ma'am, they reply in unison.

"Good!" I say sternly. Thankfully, they've stopped grilling me about Erin and have returned to their usual banter and biting remarks toward each other, leaving me out of it.

On the drive, I can't help but be charmed by the beauty of the hills and mountains still covered with snow. Looking toward the Atlantic, I see small vessels docked at the piers. The rocky shoreline breaks the gray, cold, and choppy waves that crash against it. It's simply breathtaking and will be the perfect backdrop for this photo shoot.

Smiling, I close my eyes and, as I often do, mentally frame shots of the models in the foreground of this picturesque town. But those thoughts quickly fade, replaced by images of my lovely and beautiful Erin.

CHAPTER 4

ERIN

After securing and tying down the Beechcraft, I'm heading to *The Lexington Inn* by taxi. As I gaze at the beautiful landscape and the breathtaking coastal views, my mind drifts to Laura. I can't help but smile, knowing she wants me in her life again, though a sense of anxiety lingers.

I recall that intimate moment we shared in her darkroom late one evening. We had spent so much time together, and I had fallen in love with her long before that intimate moment of holding her in my arms. Many times, I've reconsidered my decision to kiss her. I should have realized that she couldn't envision us as more than intimate friends, as she called it, given that I was only nineteen.

Laura has always been so morally ethical, so I should have realized it, but in that moment, I felt she wanted me. She did want me, but her moral code prevented her from moving beyond those intimate kisses we shared that evening in her darkroom. No matter how strong our connection was, she wouldn't allow herself to cross that line with a 19-year-old woman—even if that woman was me.

CHAPTER 4

Traveling along Route 1, I replay the morning that I took off in my beat-up plane, distraught and depressed. I was still haunted by the pain of losing Laura, even after two years. The hurt clung to my heart, refusing to let go.

I knew the weather wasn't ideal for flying, but I didn't care. Flying had been my escape, a way to distance myself from the anguish of our separation. Waking that morning after a night of crying, I felt a desperate need to get up into the clouds, hoping that being above it all would help soothe the pain in my heart.

Flying that morning did lift my spirits until the fog rolled in, and then everything went wrong. As I became disoriented, a rush of adrenaline surged through my system, amplifying my struggle to maintain any sense of direction or spatial awareness.

Suddenly, a violent jolt rocked the plane as it crashed into the treetops. The deafening sound of branches snapping and popping further disoriented me. At that moment, a chilling realization swept over me—I felt my life was unraveling. The cockpit vibrated intensely, and the once-familiar controls seemed to slip out of reach. My heartbeat pounded in my ears, drowning out any hope of regaining control as chaos enveloped me.

As the plane struck the marshland with a nearly crushing force, I saw Laura's beautiful face flash before me amid the chaos of the breaking aircraft. The violent jerks and the pressure against my seat were overwhelming, and then I fell into a void of complete darkness.

Suddenly, the darkness receded, giving way to a bright, loving light that guided me to a stunning, brilliant coastline. I scooped up a handful of pure white sand, holding it high and letting it cascade through my fingers with laughter.

As I laughed, a tender voice behind me asked, "What are you doing, *My Beautiful Girl?*" I recognized Laura's voice instantly. I gathered another handful of pure white sand and turned to face her, tossing it into the air, where it shimmered and seemed to vanish into the bright light.

Laura laughed at me, then reached out her hand, and I took it with a smile, feeling a profound sense of peace. She and I walked the beautiful, brilliant coastline, smiling at one another. There was no need to speak because, in that enchanting moment, I felt her love for me and knew she did indeed desire me.

That beautiful and loving dream became my solace over the next year as I healed from the plane crash. The knowledge that Laura truly desired me was a profound comfort for my emotional and physical wounds. I clung to that vivid dream, finding reassurance in the belief that one day, Laura would return to me. And now, she has, just as the dream foretold.

Entering *the Lexington Inn*, I'm overwhelmed by the grandeur of the expansive lobby and the dark polished hardwood floor that shines beneath the light of the elegant hanging chandeliers. The chandeliers illuminate the lobby in a soft, golden glow.

Suddenly, I see Laura standing in front of the burning grand fireplace with a warm and inviting fire. She turns toward me and smiles. She is absolutely breathtaking as the warm glow of the fire lights up her dark hair and one side of her face.

She stands waiting for me to approach her, and all I can do is smile and walk toward the woman I've always loved more than anything on this earth. "You made it," she says sweetly.

"Yes, I did. Were you waiting for me?" I ask softly.

"Of course I was," she replies, holding my eyes. Things get quiet between us as we remain in this enchanted moment. Something in the way she is looking at me has prompted me to touch her back. Laura closes her eyes for a brief moment at my touch, then she opens them and turns her gaze to the fire.

Still looking into the fire, she says, "I have your key for you." Turning back and facing me she adds, "Our rooms are upstairs on the mezzanine. Would you like to go up?"

"Yes, that would be nice," I reply with a smile.

Walking the steps to the mezzanine, we remain silent until we reach the end of one of the long hallways. Laura hands me my key and says, "You're in room 210, and I'm in room 208 next to you. "

"Taking the key, I can't help but grin and feel a bit shy. "Thank you for putting me next to you, Laura."

She catches my hand and looks at me confidently, saying, "I want you next to me, Erin. Just like old times."

"I think dinner in the dining hall is between 6 and 8. I need to contact Helena Fitzgerald; she's the art director for Victor Voss. But you and I will definitely have dinner together," Laura says with a smile.

"You're shooting Victor Voss!?" I ask in a surprising tone.

She laughs and says, "Yes. They have been one of my major clients for the past five years. They are demanding as hell, but they also pay very well."

"Laura, are you sure you shouldn't have dinner with her and discuss the photo shoot?"

"Interlacing her fingers with mine, Laura replies, "I typically do, but they don't own me until tomorrow. So tonight, I'll spend my evening however I wish."

An immediate rush of tender pain courses through every nerve, building intensity until it reaches my feminine core, where it settles into a deep erotic sensation. Gazing into her eyes, I smile and say, "Thank you, that makes me happy. I'll be in my room until then. I want to bathe and change clothes. Just knock on my door when you're ready."

"Okay, I'll knock around 6 or 6:30," she replies, kissing my cheek where my scar is. Then she adds, "I want to know more about this scar and how it's impacted you, Erin."

I nod, looking down, and softly say, "Okay." As Laura releases me, I enter my room and immediately collapse onto the bed. After that tender kiss and her desire to understand how the crash has affected me, I feel completely vulnerable.

Walking into the bathroom, I spot the inviting white porcelain clawfoot tub, its elegance drawing me in. I turn on the warm water, watching it fill the tub as I begin to undress, my eyes fixed on my reflection in the expansive mirror above the vanity.

Standing completely nude as the water continues to rise, I gaze at the scars that trace across my chest, stomach, and down my arms—remnants of the crash that changed everything. Turning to examine the one on my back, my emotions churn.

That scar, the deepest, was from the jagged metal of the plane as it tore apart just before slicing into my flesh. The pain from that moment lingers most vividly, as it was this wound that plunged me into darkness.

Stepping into the tub, I am suddenly overwhelmed by a wave of emotion, and I begin to cry uncontrollably. The memories of that horrific incident flood back, and I feel a deep sorrow for how it has transformed my once youthful body into something I now perceive as grotesque. A new fear grips me—what if Laura finds my body ugly? She always called me her "*Beautiful Girl.*" But now, if she sees me, I'm sure she won't be able to ever say that again.

CHAPTER 5

LAURA

Tossing another log onto the fire in my room's fireplace, I stand and watch the flames immediately wrap around the fresh piece of wood. Sitting back in the chair facing the fire, I pick up the phone and call the front desk.

Good afternoon; this is Joan at the front desk. How may I assist you?"

"Hello Joan, this is Miss Lomax in room 208. Would you ring Helena Fitzgerald's room for me, please,"

"Yes, Miss Lomax. One moment, please."

"Hello," Helena says.

"Hi, Helena. Well, here we are again."

"Laura! It's so good to hear your voice, and yes, here we are again. Can you believe it's already been a year?"

"No, time gets away from us, doesn't it?"

"Yes, and now here I am one year older. Well, time ages all of us."

"Hey, speak for yourself," I say in jest. Then add, "I decided last January when I turned 50 that I would have no more birthdays. So I will remain eternally 50," I say as I laugh.

"You're 51, Laura? That's impossible; you don't look a day over 40, and I am being sincere."

"Oh Helena, hush. You're well aware of my age. But I love your flattery."

We both continue making small talk, intermingled with laughter. Then Helena says, "Are we having dinner tonight as usual, Laura?"

They are paying me, so I always feel obligated to join the models and Helena for dinner, but she has become a close friend over the years, so I want to be honest with her.

"About that, Helena," I say and pause.

"Is something wrong, Laura?"

"Oh no, but I've made dinner plans with someone else," I reply anxiously.

"Who is she?" Helena asks, her voice tinged with amusement.

"Dammit, Helena. I haven't been with anyone in years. How could you possibly know this?"

"Woman's intuition, my dear," she replies with a chuckle. "Now, go ahead, spill it."

"Well, there's nothing really to spill. But okay, I know you're my friend and very discreet, so I'll just say it." I pause for a moment, gathering my thoughts.

Helena says, "I would normally say, just tell me when you're ready, but you've got my curiosity piqued, honey."

"Okay, here it goes. The pilot who flew us in is very special to me. She was and still is my favorite model, and we became very close years ago. It wasn't sexual, but it was emotionally intense. Over the past year, I learned she owns an aviation business, so I asked her to fly us to Maine."

"Wow, Laura. How old is she?"

"She's 30 now," I reply hesitantly.

"How old was she when you fell in love with her, Laura?"

"Nothing sexual ever happened between us, Helena!" I say firmly.

"That isn't what I asked you, Laura," she responds softly.

"Helena, this isn't something I've admitted to anyone." I gaze into the fire, replaying the memory of that day she was in my arms, and I was loving her.

"Laura, listen. You're a beautiful woman with one flaw that makes you a great person but also precludes you from being human at times. You're ethical to a fault. So I'll ask you again—how old was she when you fell in love with her?"

Hesitantly, I admit, "She was nineteen." And I begin to cry.

"What room are you in?" Helena asks.

"208," I tell her through my tears. After hanging up, I grab a tissue to dry my eyes. Moments later, there's a soft knock on my door.

Opening my door, I see Helena dressed in black and looking stunning as always. She enters, pulls me into a hug, and I start crying uncontrollably.

"Laura, come over here and sit by the fire."

Sitting beside her, I say, "God, I feel foolish."

"Well, I would say that's a step in the right direction, Laura," she says, reaching for my hand.

"Helena, I want you to know I'll have all this under control by tomorrow morning when we start our first location shoot."

"Oh dear lord, Laura. There you go again. Just when I thought you were making a little progress, you want to stuff all this love and these feelings back into a box and revert to being Miss Ethical and stoic." She holds my hand between both of hers.

"Honey, I know you're a pro when you have that camera in your hands, and nothing short of the end of the world would deter you from staying focused and professional on set."

"I shouldn't have asked her to fly us here; I'm a complete mess," I tell Helena, my gaze fixed on the flames that have entirely engulfed the log I threw in a few moments ago.

Helena's eyes meet mine. "Are you still in love with her, Laura?"

I hold Helena's gaze and nod, tears streaming down my face. "I should have just called her instead of disguising my desire to see her by hiring her. That was foolish," I say, irritated with myself.

Helena chuckles softly, and then I join her. "Laura, you could have saved yourself years of heartache if you had done one thing."

Curiously, I ask, "What's that?"

"The glaringly obvious, Laura!" She replies in frustration. She looks me squarely in the eyes and says, "You should have slept with her."

I shake my head. "I couldn't do that."

"Why not, Laura? I bet she was, and still is, crazy in love with you, and I haven't even met her." Helena gazes at the fire and asks, "Is she still in love with you, Laura?"

Meeting Helena's eyes again, I feel the tears pooling and whisper, "Yes, I can feel it from her."

"Then why are you crying?" Helena says with a giggle.

"Hell, I don't know."

"Look, you lost her once; do you want to lose her again?" Helena asks seriously.

I nod resolutely and say, "No, I never want to know another day without her."

Helena smiles and says, "See, it's that simple. The two of you are still in love, so why are you making it difficult?"

"Because I know I hurt her badly. One day, while we were in the darkroom, she kissed me, and I didn't resist at first. I held her in my arms and loved her, but then guilt over-whelmed me because of her age. After that, we tried to talk about it, but I pushed her away, believing she would be better off without me. I mean, my god, Helena. I was forty, and she was nineteen."

"Is this the same woman you mentioned to me five years ago that you couldn't get over?"

"Yes, it is indeed," I reply, shaking my head.

"Laura, my gosh honey, you haven't got over her in all these years?"

"No. I haven't been able to move past it. I loved Erin so much."

Helena is silent for a moment, and then she retakes my hand. "Laura, she flew you and your crew up here and is staying with you, right?"

I nod. "Yes, next door." I point toward her room.

Helena bursts into laughter. "You put her next to you? Damn, you are making progress." Tilting her head toward a door on the other side of the fireplace, she adds, "You realize that door can be opened from both sides." Then she giggles.

My mouth opens, and I look back at Helena, blushing deeply. "Oh, good heavens," I say, covering my face with my hands.

Fussing with my hair as I glance in the bathroom mirror, I notice it's almost 6 o'clock. I chose my favorite high-waisted black slacks and a white cardigan over a silk blouse. I gave up dresses years ago but always ensure my attire remains stylish. After applying my red lipstick, I lean in to scrutinize the fine lines on my face. They are what they are, I think to myself.

Standing back, I gaze at my reflection, taking a moment to truly see the woman staring back at me. Leaning toward the mirror, I try to find myself in the reflection. Speaking softly, I say, "You have lived without her all these years. Don't be a damn fool for another eleven years."

With that, I walk out of my room and knock softly on Erin's door. Taking a deep breath, I exhale slowly and wait for Erin to answer.

Opening the door, I see her and gasp. "You look amazing, Erin," I say breathlessly.

"Thank you, Laura. Come in; you look stunning as usual," she says with a smile.

Walking into the room, I immediately notice the fire-place's warm and inviting fire crackling. The walls are painted a deep seaside blue, reminiscent of colonial times. A massive wool rug covers almost the entire floor, stretching from under the bed and flowing out to the fireplace.

Turning back to Erin, I say, "You're so beautiful, Erin, just as you've always been."

Erin responds softly, "Thank you, Laura. After the plane crash, I haven't felt that way, but I know you're sincere, so that means a lot."

I walk to her, take her hands in mine, and look into her soft, earthy-green eyes. "You're even more beautiful, Erin. You truly are "My *Beautiful Girl*." I've said it! That's what I used to call her. If I want Erin, I know I need to prove my love. I know that Erin still loves me, but does she trust me with her heart?

Her eyes glisten as we hold hands and remain close. "It seems like a lifetime since I've heard that from you, Laura."

Touching her cheek, I gaze into her eyes and say, "Well, it won't be the last time." Erin grins and pulls me close, offering me a warm and tender hug.

"You're still so gorgeous, Laura. And I have indeed missed you," she whispers, holding me tenderly.

Wanting her to feel my love, I tighten my embrace and inhale her intoxicating perfume. "You smell amazing, Erin."

Suddenly, I feel her fingers threading through my hair as she pulls me closer. "Are you ready for dinner?" she asks tenderly.

"Yes, but I don't want to release you," I reply.

"Neither do I, Laura," she whispers.

Taking a deep breath, I softly say, "I was a damn fool, Erin." She releases me and gazes into my eyes, nodding in understanding.

"Well, I should have been braver and more persistent and not let you go so easily. I regret that."

"Let's go out for dinner, Erin. I know we could have our own table in the dining hall, but I don't want our first evening together interrupted by Mark, Julie, and the whole crew. I'll see enough of them over the next few days."

Erin beams at me and says, "I love that idea. I saw a place on the ride from the airport. Let me quickly call a taxi, and then we can head out. Is that alright?"

"That sounds lovely, Erin. Yes, please arrange it for us."

After Erin finishes the call, she says, "They said they'll be here in about 20 minutes, so please, take a seat, Laura."

Like mine, her room has two chairs by the fireplace. We sit together in quietness, watching the flickering flames. I break the silence by asking, "What prompted you to pursue flying?"

With a chuckle, Erin turns toward me and responds, "Well, after leaving modeling, I tried college, but my only real talent was playing poker in the student lounge."

I laugh and say, "Somehow, I can imagine that, Erin."

She continues, "College wasn't for me, but one morning, I was driving and saw a plane flying overhead. I got a wild idea and started chasing it. The road was empty, so I was only concerned once I reached about 80 miles per hour.

Realizing my car couldn't catch up, I pulled over and stepped out to watch. To my surprise, the pilot must have noticed me. The plane made a graceful turn and flew low overhead, its engines roaring as it passed. I waved, and the pilot turned around again, making another pass, leaving me in awe.

Energized, I jumped back into my car and raced to the airport. To my amazement, the same plane was taxiing toward me. I approached the plane, and he greeted me with a big smile when I looked into the pilot's window.

His name was John Carpenter, and for the next six months, he taught me everything he knew about flying."

"Erin, that's such an amazing story," I say, genuinely in awe of her bravery. "You said his name *was* John."

"Yes," she replies softly. Unfortunately, John passed away about five years ago. He and I became very close; he was like a second dad to me. He was always so generous with his time and knowledge. I wouldn't be where I am now without John." As she speaks, I notice her eyes glisten in the firelight.

"I'm so sorry you lost your friend, Erin," I say, my voice filled with sympathy.

"Thank you, Laura," she replies. Then she stands and walks to the window, peering out for a moment. Turning back to me, she extends her hand, and I take it and stand to meet her.

"Come on, our taxi is here," she says with a warm smile. Then she leans in and kisses my cheek softly. I can't help but grin, entirely charmed by Erin's tenderness and excitement about our date.

As we reach the door to leave, I pull her into a loving hug and kiss her cheek. Smiling into those earthy-green eyes—the same eyes I fell in love with years ago—I feel a familiar warmth in my heart.

CHAPTER 6

ERIN

Laura and I had a wonderful dinner, and now we're in the taxi on our way back to *The Lexington Inn*. "It's bitterly cold up here," Laura says as she shivers. Taking her cold hands between mine, I warm them. "How do you have such warm hands in this weather, Erin?"

Chuckling, I reply, "It's one of the few positives from my accident. Isn't that odd?" I ask with a grin.

"Well, it's a benefit that I plan on taking full advantage of," Laura says as she moves closer. Smiling at her, I continue warming her bitterly cold hands with mine. It's only about 8 o'clock, Erin. What would you like to do?"

Gazing into her deep brown eyes, which my heart fell for years ago, I whisper, "Just be with you, Laura. I don't care what we do."

Laura pulls my hands to her lips and kisses them sweetly. "Will you come to my room so you and I can spend more time together?" She asks as she gazes sweetly at me.

"Yes, I'd love that, Laura."

As we walk up the stairs to the Mezzanine, a beautiful blonde about Laura's age approaches us. She smiles at Laura and glances at me, offering me a smile as well. "Hi, Helena. This is my dear friend, Erin Winslow, whom I spoke with you about earlier. She's always been my favorite model, even though she gave it up years ago.

"Hello, Erin. It's wonderful to meet you." She gazes at me and adds, "It's too bad you gave up modeling, Erin because you are handsomely gorgeous."

"Thank you, Helena, that's very kind. I appreciate you letting me steal Laura away from you for dinner tonight."

Helena glances at Laura with a grin that seems to grow mischievous. She loops her arm through mine and says, "You didn't steal her, Erin. Laura flat-out told me she wasn't having dinner with me because she wanted to be with you."

Laura looks a bit embarrassed, but I give Helena a grin and play along. "What else did she tell you, Helena?" I ask playfully and chuckle.

Helena laughs. Looking at Laura, she says, "I like her, Laura. She has an earthy grit about her." Then she gazes back at me and adds, "If you get tired of Laura, honey, look me up." We all chuckle.

Feeling embarrassed, I smile at Laura, who looks even more so.

"Helena, you're a mess!" Laura says. Then asks, "Where is everyone?"

"Well, Mark is 'holding court' in the dining hall with all the models and my crew, as usual; Julie is also down there. I just let the young ones have it; I'm tired, so I'm headed to my room for the evening."

"I'm assuming the charter bus will pick us all up at 5:30 in the morning as usual? Laura asks Helena.

"Yes, it will. And breakfast will be at 5 a.m. in the dining hall for all of us. So I'll see you in the morning, sweetie," Helena tells Laura, then hugs her and whispers something in her ear.

"It was lovely to meet you, Helena," I say as I gaze at her and smile.

Taking my hand between hers, she says, "It's so nice to meet you, Erin, and I'm glad you're with us for the next few days. Whatever magic you have over Laura, please keep it up because I've never seen her glow like this."

"I intend to, Helena." I bravely assert.

She looks at Laura, winks, and then bids us goodnight.

As we continue down the corridor to our rooms, Laura says, "I'm sorry if she embarrassed you, Erin. Helena always speaks her mind no matter what."

"Somewhat, but I think she embarrassed you a lot more," I say with a grin.

Laura stops at our doors and says, "Well, she did, but everything she said is true."

Entering Laura's room, I see that the firelight is dimming, so I put two logs on the fire and begin to work with it. "Would you like some wine, Erin?"

"Yes, that would be nice, Laura," I reply as I continue poking the fire.

Laura walks to the phone, calls the dining hall, and orders a bottle of chardonnay. Then she walks back to me and begins warming her hands with the intense heat of the fire. "Have a seat, Erin."

"Okay, but let me go next door and put a couple of logs in my fireplace, and then I'll be right back." Laura gazes at me intensely, then walks over to a door on the other side of the fireplace and unlocks it, smiling at me.

"I would love it if you came back through here, Erin?" She asked with her eyes still fixed on me intensely.

Nodding with a grin, I walk to her entry door and look back at her. "Yes, I'll only be a minute." My grin grows wide as I quickly enter my room, place another log on my fire, and walk to the door connecting mine and Laura's room.

Before I unlock the door, I quickly walk to the bathroom mirror, fuss with my hair, look at my scar, and become somber and anxious.

As I open the adjoining door, I see Laura standing in front of the fireplace, illuminated by the soft glow of the fire-light and a single lamp. She looks at me seriously and asks, "Erin, what's wrong, darling?"

"Nothing," I say sharply.

"Erin, please sit with me."

Sitting next to her, I peer into the firelight and try to quickly pull myself out of the gloominess that comes over me sometimes in an instant when I catch a glimpse of myself in the mirror.

"Talk to me, Erin?" Laura whispers sweetly.

Nodding my head, I say, "I just glanced at myself in the mirror. Sometimes darkness engulfs me when I see my face." Laura reaches for my hands and holds them.

"I can understand how that would affect you, Erin. Darling, I could tell you a thousand times how beautiful you are, but I know that wouldn't scare away the darkness you feel. Is there anything I can do to help?" She asks me with a loving gaze.

Suddenly, we hear a knock on the door. Rising, I say, "I'll get it, Laura." As I walk back toward the table, I set the bucket with the bottle of wine on it and begin opening it. Laura encircles me from behind, hugging me intimately. I'm over-come by fear and excitement as Laura's love envelops me.

"Turning toward her, I immediately ask, "Why couldn't you love me like this years ago, Laura?!" She looks slightly shocked at my question but holds my gaze.

"That's a good question, Erin," she replies, then adds, "Please pour us both a glass and then come and sit next to me by the fire."

As I pour the wine, I feel lingering fear and an unexpected

anger toward her. I thought I had forgiven Laura, but now I'm questioning it. I walk over, hand her a glass, and sit in the chair beside her.

"Laura, I know I was only nineteen, but you and I were in love, and you dare not deny that."

Laura sips her wine, then looks at me and reaches for my hand. I take it as I gaze at her. "Erin, you are right. I deeply loved you, but darling, it was hard to admit. Erin, I was 40 years old."

Gazing into the fire, I say, "Laura, I'm 30 now, and I realize I probably wouldn't be able to get involved with a nineteen-year-old at my age, so I can understand the difficulty you faced. However, you allowed yourself to become emotionally intimate with me, so I don't see why you wouldn't allow me in your bed."

Laura sits back in her chair and gazes into the firelight. She stays silent as she sips her wine, then leans toward me and softly says, "You were in my bed every night, Erin."

My anger flares at her remark—well-intentioned, maybe, but it hits like salt in a wound. I shoot to my feet and shout, "Goddammit, Laura, what's the difference? You *hurt* me!" My voice cracks, and I feel the sting of tears before I can hold them back. I storm out of her room, retreat to mine, and collapse into the chair by the fireplace. I grab my wine and take a deep, furious swig, allowing the anger to rise. I down the entire glass, each gulp fueling the fire within me.

Laura enters my room and asks, "May I sit, Erin."

Nodding, I simply say, "Yes," as I continue gazing into the firelight. Laura walks back into her room and quickly rejoins me with the bottle of wine. Holding my glass to her, she refills it and then sits in the chair beside me as we remain quiet.

"Laura, sitting here with you, I don't understand why I'm this enraged. Perhaps it's because I saw my reflection moments ago, which stirred up emotions. I flew out that morning because of the pain I still felt from losing you. I'm not blaming you for my accident; that's entirely my fault. It was foolish to fly that morning."

Gazing at Laura, her eyes are locked onto mine with deep intensity. "You have every right to be angry at me, Erin," she says, her voice steady yet remorseful. "I should have taken you to my bed every chance I could. You're right—I fantasized about you constantly, so what the hell was the difference?" She confesses, her gaze drifting back to the fire.

After several moments of silence, Laura turns toward me and says, "Erin, I'm 51 years old now, and I'm still very much in love with you. If you can forgive me, I'd like to try with you now, at this age."

Gazing into Laura's dark eyes, which have haunted me for years, I softly ask, "Are you still in love with me, Laura?"

"Very much so, Erin. And now, I feel I'm allowed to have you if you still want me," she says bravely. Then she asks, "Erin, do you still love me?"

Glancing back at the fire, I reply, "Laura, I've never stopped loving you, and yes, I am still very much in love with you."

As Laura gazes at me with a smile, she takes my wine and sets our glasses on the fireplace mantel. With a grin, she stands at my chair and attempts to sit on my lap. Pulling her to me, I immediately grab her tightly and ask, "This is completely out of your comfort zone, Miss Lomax. Is this the new and improved Laura?" I ask with a chuckle.

Looking into my eyes, she says, "Yes, Erin. I won't be a fool any longer. I've waited eleven years for you and am tired of waiting."

"My god, Laura, why did it take so long?" I say, shaking my head as I peer back at the fire.

"I was waiting for you to grow up, *My Beautiful Girl*," she replies, resting against me with a sigh. Holding her close, I inhale her familiar scent, the same smell I remember from years ago. I was so young then, but completely in love with Laura.

"Laura?" I whisper.

"Yes, Erin."

"Had you given us a chance, I'd still be with you. But my head tells me you made the right decision about not becoming sexually involved with me, but at times, I've been so angry at you for pushing me away."

Laura looks into the firelight. "I don't blame you, Erin. I felt it was best if we severed ties because, as we've both admitted, we were very much in love, and I didn't know how to be with you after kissing and loving you that night in the darkroom." Turning back to me, she looks into my eyes and adds, "Erin, at that moment, I wanted to take you to my bed and make love to you, baby," she confesses, tears welling up in her eyes. Pulling her to me, I hold her as she cries. Tearfully, she whispers, "I wanted you so badly, Erin."

Holding her tightly, I gaze into the fire and whisper, "Laura, I wanted you at that moment. And god, yes, I wanted you to take me to your bed, I craved you, Laura. No other woman has ever reached the places in me that you have."

Laura whispers, "Do you think it's too late for us, Erin?"

"If you and I waited another eleven years, it would never be too late for us, Laura. And perhaps It was for the best because the love and passion I feel for you now can't even compare to what the nineteen-year-old Erin felt."

CHAPTER 7

LAURA

As Erin holds me close, I feel an intense peace—the same contentment I found with her years ago. "You comfort me, Erin. You always did," I whisper.

Still cradling me in her lap, Erin scoots to the edge of her chair, holding me tightly. I give her a puzzled look and a familiar mischievous grin spreads across her face. Suddenly, she tightens her grip and stands with me in her arms. I grab my glass of wine, and Erin gently tosses me onto the bed.

Laughing loudly, I try not to spill my wine as I look at her in amazement and ask, "What are you doing?" Erin crawls onto the bed beside me and pulls me close.

"I'm going to finish that kiss I started in the darkroom eleven years ago," she replies, taking my glass and setting it on the side table.

Erin moves on top of me, her lovely earthy-green eyes locking with mine. As the fire crackles and pops in the background, our lips reunite. Her tender kiss is just as I remember it, only sweeter. I wrap my arms around her neck, pulling her close as our hungry mouths rediscover each other.

As I open my lips, I feel my lovely Erin, *My Beautiful Girl* from a decade ago, loving me with an erotic passion and a growing lust. I tenderly thread my fingers through her familiar brown locks, hair I've touched many times. But now, I no longer wish to soothe her—I want to own her. I pull her tight, matching her passion as my heart surges with a tender ache, and my body pulses with an erotic desire for her.

I push against her warm tongue with mine, the very sensation I've longed for and loved in my fantasies. I fully embrace this lovely young woman from my past—the woman who lit up my world years ago.

Pulling away, I grip Erin's hair and look into those lovely eyes that have haunted me for over a decade. As I gaze into her eyes, I see the young Erin I once knew, and suddenly, the weight of losing her overwhelms me, and the lonely, painful years without her begin to drip from my eyes.

Erin holds me close, her own tears joining mine. Our emotions are raw, still wounded from the vastness of the time that separated us. As I pull her even closer, I feel my young Erin grieving with me. With tears in my eyes, I thread my fingers through her thick brown hair again and whisper, "I love you, *My Beautiful Girl.*"

Erin falls to my side, sobbing, whispering my name, "Laura, Laura." I rise above her and gaze at her tear-streaked face.

Gently touching her cheek, I softly say, "I'm still so in love with you, Erin. I haven't loved anyone since you."

Erin's cries gradually ease as she looks back at me with disbelief. "You haven't loved anyone since me, Laura?" she asks, her voice filled with uncertainty.

I look at her perfect lips, then back into the depths of her tender soul. "How could I possibly have loved anyone else, Erin?" I reply, my voice full of sincerity.

She touches my face with her hands, then threads her

fingers tenderly through my hair as she searches my eyes, wanting to believe my words. Through her tears, Erin smiles and pulls me gently to her sweet lips.

Erin kisses me softly, her lips tender and full of love, her soul graceful and beautiful. As our lips part, our tongues meet delicately, pushing against one another. Erin gently sucks my tongue, and I feel my heart and body pulse with a painful warmth. The tenderness of her touch makes me weak, and I realize just how incredible it is to have Erin loving me again.

Releasing my tongue gently, she kisses my lips sweetly before pulling away. "My gosh, Erin, you're incredible," I say as I fall back against the bed. Erin giggles, and I join her, our laughter filling the room as we revel in the joy of being together again, breathing the same air again.

Crawling on top of her and straddling her, I sit and gaze down at my lovely Erin, who still loves me. We clasp hands, our laughter slowly fading as the emotional weight of the moment settles in.

Gazing down at her, she softly asks, "Will you stay with me tonight, Laura."

Smiling, I nod and kiss her hands gently. "Yes, darling, I want to sleep beside you all night."

"Laura, it's too soon to be sexually intimate, but sleeping next to you all night will be almost as good, baby."

"Yes, it will, and I agree, it's too soon for intimacy. But Erin, I'll make love to you anytime you ask me. If you asked me now, I'd take you to my bed and make love to you tenderly all night long."

Grinning at me, Erin says, "I love the sound of that."

Gently lowering myself onto her, I smile and kiss her lips softly. "Perhaps it would be best if we slept in my room in case someone needs me. Is that okay?"

"Of course, I don't care where we sleep. We could sleep

with Helena as long as I'm completely snuggled against you, Laura."

Laughing loudly, I reply, "My gosh, Erin, that's funny. Helena would love that. You obviously don't know her like I do."

Pulling away slightly and giving me a curious look, she simply asks, "Helena?"

"Oh gosh, no, Erin!" I say. But she did try the first year I began shooting for Victor Voss."

"Oh really? Tell me about that?"

Resting my head against Erin, I giggle as she waits with an expectant look. "Darling, I don't remember the exact details."

"Helena's a gorgeous woman, Laura," she replies, curiosity piqued.

Rising to sit beside her on the bed, I say, "She and I found ourselves in an intimate closeness one evening after drinks." As I look at Erin, she's clearly waiting for more, so I continue. "Helena leaned in and kissed me. I was in total shock, but I tried to be tender and kind. So I simply said something like, *'Helena, you're a beautiful woman, but I'm still in pain from a breakup that I can't seem to get past.'*"

Erin looks at me, puzzled. "But that was five years ago, Laura. Who were you trying to get over?"

Feeling tears pooling in my eyes, I see Erin's expression shift from confusion to a tender understanding. She sits up, pulls me close, and whispers, "Laura, even after all these years?"

Nodding against her, I whisper, "I'm still not over you, Erin." Pulling away slightly, I add, "That's why I called you. I've wanted you back in my life for so long, and I couldn't wait any longer. I had no idea if you were with someone; I just prayed that you weren't."

Erin's gaze meets mine, and she asks, "What if I had been with someone now, Laura?"

Expelling a nervous chuckle, I look at her intently and respond, "Then she would have had a hell of a fight on her hands," Erin."

Laughing, Erin grabs me and pulls me close. "I like that answer, and I love this side of you, Laura. You really would have fought for me?"

Nodding, I reply, "You better believe it, Erin. You're mine, and you always have been." Leaning in, I kiss her lips tenderly, then add, "And you always will be."

"Come here, baby, Erin says sweetly as she pulls me against her."

As Erin holds me, I close my eyes and listen to the crackling of the fire and her tender heart beating. Reaching around her, I snuggle close.

After a few moments of loving silence, Erin says, "I'm ready for bed, Laura."

Smiling, I whisper, "So am I, darling."

After changing into my nightgown, I see Erin walking back into my room through the adjoining door. Smiling at her, I begin pulling the bedding back. "Let me help," she says sweetly.

"What time do you have to get up, Laura?"

"Probably around 4 a.m. to shower and dress because breakfast is at 5 o'clock. I don't expect you to get up that early, darling," I say as I get under the covers and turn toward her. Erin is still standing beside the bed in her pajamas, making me smile.

"Why are you smiling," She asks with a grin.

"You. You're adorable in those pajamas," I reply as I reach out for her. Erin crawls beside me, and I pull her close before rising above her. Threading my fingers through her soft, dark hair, I whisper, "My bed will always be open for you, Erin."

She gives me a tender gaze, touches my cheek, and looks at my lips. "I still remember how you tasted that night in the darkroom, Laura. The smell of the photo chemicals filled the air and mingled with your scent. The warm glow of the amber light illuminated you, and that moment cast an overpowering spell over me."

Gazing into Erin's eyes, I touch her lips and whisper, "I felt it too, and I signaled that I wanted you.

Something magical happened when you put your arms around me and kissed me. The Erin I loved so much engulfed me, and my love for you turned into pure lust.

I did fantasize about you, as I've confessed, but up until that kiss, I had loved you sweetly and tenderly. But as we loved one another in that moment, an overwhelming erotic passion began to burn intensely, and that's when I became overwhelmingly frightened."

"Why, Laura?"

"I'm not sure, Erin. Maybe I was ashamed by the many erotic fantasies I'd had about you and realized that's where they had to remain—simply fantasies."

Erin pulls me to her and softly says, "I understand, Laura...You need to sleep now, baby. I know how grueling these shoots are. Goodnight, love."

Snuggling against her, I whisper, "Good night, *My Beautiful Girl.*"

CHAPTER 8

ERIN

I wake up the following day to the warmth of Laura's gentle kiss on my lips. Smiling, I open my eyes and see her beautiful face illuminated by the fire's soft glow.

"Are you leaving now?" I ask, my voice still heavy with sleep.

Sitting beside me, she replies, "Yes, darling. It's almost 5:30, so we'll all be heading out soon. I let the kitchen staff know you'd be down for breakfast sometime before nine."

"I'll get up before then, but thank you.".

"Damn, you're so hard to leave," she says as she threads her fingers through my hair. "I love you, Erin. You've always been the love of my life."

"Laura," I whisper with a smile.

"I'll see you around 10 o'clock. As you know, I won't shoot past nine because of the lighting."

"Yes, I know. What time will you resume shooting this afternoon?" I ask as I touch her face.

"Around 3 o'clock, most likely. I'll need to spend some time with Helena to review the shoot list, but we can have lunch in the dining hall if you'd like."

"Of course, I would. Go ahead, baby, and please don't fret over me today; I'll keep myself busy."

Laura kisses me tenderly, then whispers, "You felt so good next to me all night, baby."

Kissing her cheek, I reply, "I love you, Laura. I'll see you soon." As she leaves, I pull her pillow to me and inhale her scent. A million emotions rush through my mind and soul—love, lust, vulnerability, and compassion—all vexed together in one ball of complexity. However, the one lucid emotion that genuinely matters is that I love Laura with an over-whelming depth that is timeless and unwavering.

After breakfast, I settle into a cozy chair in the front lounge by the large stone fireplace—where Laura was waiting for me yesterday. Gazing into the firelight, my thoughts remain on Laura and how wonderful her warm body felt beside me all night as I slept peacefully.

Lost in thought, I suddenly feel a cold breeze from the front door opening. Glancing toward the entry door, I see Helena walking in with an unsteady young woman.

Walking toward them, I ask, "Do you need some help, Helena?"

"Thank you, Erin. This is Amy, one of our models. She's having an onset of vertigo." After I say hello to her, I help Helena steady her.

"Thank you, Erin. Will you please help me take her to her room?"

As we walk Amy down the corridor, she keeps repeating, "I'm sorry, Helena."

"Honey, it's okay. I have bouts of vertigo at times and know how debilitating it can be. You just need to go to bed, and hopefully, it will subside."

After we get Amy into her bed, Helena sits beside her, holding her hand, assuring her that she will be okay.

"May I get anything from the dining hall, Helena?"

Helena turns toward me, smiles, and replies, "Yes, Erin, please get a pitcher of ice water."

"Yes, of course. I'll be right back." After I get the water, I return quickly to Amy's room and set the pitcher of water and a glass on her side table.

Helena catches my hand and says, "Thank you, sweetie." I smile and nod at her, then leave the room, returning to my chair by the fireplace.

As I sip my coffee, I realize how being down a model might upset the shooting. Since the model is fitted specifically for each outfit, this can affect not only wardrobe fitting issues but also scheduling delays and team morale. I can't help but worry about how this might be affecting Laura.

While I sip my coffee, I see Helena returning to the lounge and walking toward me. "Is she okay, Helena?"

"I don't know; this seems to be a bad episode. Like I told Amy, I've had bouts of vertigo, and when it comes on, it can keep me in bed for days."

"Oh gosh. Can one of the other models step into her place?"

"No, I'm afraid not. Amy is taller than the rest, and her body type is unlike any of the others," she replies in frustration. She sits in the chair adjacent to me and peers into the fire.

We both sit quietly for a moment. I don't know what to say to Helena, so I sit quietly, knowing her brain is most likely scrambling to find a solution. After a moment, she turns and stares at me blankly, her expression unreadable.

"Erin?"

"Yes?" I reply.

Helena leans toward me and takes my hand as her gaze

remains fixed. Then she asks, "Erin, honey, is there any way you might consider stepping in and modeling for us?"

Looking at Helena in disbelief, I feel an overpowering discomfort and self-doubt about my ability to step back in front of the camera.

Gazing back into the fire, I softly say, "Helena, I don't know. It's been so long and...."

"I've seen your scar, Erin, and in my opinion, it makes you even more beautiful and real," Helena says tenderly.

Looking downward, I whisper, "Thank you, Helena."

"Erin, you have the same body frame and height as Amy, and it would save the shoot," she says almost pleadingly. Then she adds, "I don't know what happened to you, and I can imagine as a woman how the scar may have affected you over the years."

"Well, Helena. I would be happy if it were just the one on my face." Helena gazes at me clearly, wanting to know more.

As Helena holds my hand, tears pool in my eyes. "Helena, my entire body is scared from an airplane crash I had years ago. I felt completely ugly for a long time, and I'm really not past it.

"I'm sorry, Erin. That has to be incredibly difficult, but you are still a beauty, honey," She says sympathetically. Then asks, "What does Laura think of your scars?"

Expelling some anxiety with a chuckle, I reply, "She has only seen the same one you have seen." Helena smiles at me and remains silent as she holds my hand tenderly.

"Erin, I've never seen Laura like this. My God, it's clear that woman loves you deeply. Any scars and traumas you carry, I know she will embrace with her unique love and kindness."

Turning back to the fire, I realize I have to do this to save the shoot and myself. I don't want to, but something uncomfortable is pushing me to do this.

Looking back at Helena, I smile and nod. "Oh god, Erin. Thank you, honey. You will be amazing, and you have saved this whole shoot. No wonder Laura is crazy about you; you're one hell of a woman," she says, then chuckles.

As Helena and I travel back to the shooting location, my heart and soul are knotted with intense anxiety. Helena reaches for my hand and softly says, "It's like riding a bike, Erin. You'll find your confidence once Laura begins shooting you again."

Smiling at her, I say, "I hope so because I am terrified," I tell Helena, who is gazing at me. Something in the way she is looking at me prompts me to share more. "I'm not sure if you're aware of this, but I stopped modeling years ago because Laura couldn't accept me as her lover because of my age."

Helena pulls me close and says, "She told me yesterday, but she also admitted it was the biggest mistake of her life. And I agreed with her; I told her she was a damn fool."

We both laugh loudly. "Laura's too damn ethical, Erin. And I told her that. Honey, If you'd been interested in me, I wouldn't have had to think about it. We both laugh harder.

"You're something else, Helena," I say with laughter.

"Maybe so, but I'm also truthful. Erin, you're a gorgeous woman, and I bet you were a damn knockout at nineteen; Laura needs her head examined," She says emphatically. We both roar with laughter, which helps expel my anxiety.

Exiting the bus with Helena, I see Laura working with a model. She is entirely in her zone, and watching her work thrills me. Her fluid movements stir nostalgia in me over our tender love. My heart and stomach are filled with butterflies, battling the anxiousness I feel.

"Erin, come with me to the makeup and hair tent; it's just over here." As we enter the tent, I see two young women in their mid-30s smiling at me.

"Trudy and Liz, this is Erin. She is our new model."

"Oh goodness, girl, you're flawless," says Liz. Blushing a bit, I simply smile at her.

"Liz, you and Trudy do her hair and makeup. It shouldn't take long because you're right, Liz. Erin is indeed flawless."

"Oh hush, Helena," I say with a laugh.

As Liz works with my hair, Helena says, "I'm going to let Laura know you're here, sweetie. I don't want her to faint when you walk out there looking like a million bucks."

"Oh, you know Laura? Liz asks."

I lock eyes with Helena, who grins, then says, "Yes, that foolish Laura almost let this one get away."

"Hmmm, Liz says with a soft giggle."

After Liz finishes my makeup, Trudy begins working on my hair. She asks," So give us the low-down, Erin. How did Laura almost let you get away?"

Liz chimes in and says yeah, "Spill it, girl."

Grinning, I simply say, "I don't kiss and tell." Liz and Trudy roar with laughter. As we all laugh, Laura enters the tent with her gaze fixed on me.

"Well, hello, Laura. We hear you almost let this gorgeous creature get away from you," Trudy says with a giggle as Liz joins her. Laura looks completely embarrassed as her eyes fall back on me.

I gaze at her and simply say, "Helena."

"Ahhh, I see. Well, girls, Helena is indeed right. I was a damn fool years ago and let this one slip through my fingers, but I'll be damned if that will happen again."

"Well, let's hope not, Laura. Erin's a beauty. What in the hell were you thinking?" Liz asks.

"Obviously, I wasn't," she says, giving me a tender look. Then she asks Trudy and Liz to give us a moment together. After they leave, Laura comes close to me. "Erin, are you okay doing this? I mean, I'm sure Helena coerced you into it."

Standing, I pull Laura close and say, "I'm fine, baby. Yes, I'm nervous, but how could I let the shoot fall apart if I can help save it?"

"Oh, Erin," she murmurs softly, kissing my lips tenderly. Then she adds, "I don't know which of us will be more nervous as I photograph you, darling."

Threading my hand through her hair, I whisper, "Just look at me through your viewfinder like you used to, and you'll see me, Laura." I pull her closer and give her a tender kiss before leaning in to whisper in her ear, "I love you."

"Oh, Erin, it feels like I have my young *Beautiful Girl* back again. This feels completely magical," she says softly. Then adds, "I love you too, darling."

"You go get fitted, and I'll head back out to start shooting again. Thank you, Erin," she says, gazing into my eyes. With a wink, she turns and leaves the tent.

CHAPTER 9

LAURA

With a *'shot list'* in hand, Helena walks over to me and says, "Erin's up next." Then she gives me a warm smile.

"Erin!?" Mark exclaims with heightened excitement.

"Yes, she's taking Amy's place," Helena confirms.

"Oh gosh, look at her, Laura. She is absolutely stunning!" Mark screams with enthusiasm.

"Yes, she is, Mark!" I say as I approach her.

"Hi, darling, you are breathtaking," I say softly.

"Don't you dare make me cry, Laura! My makeup is perfect, and Trudy will kill you!" she says with a playful tone.

"Okay. I promise I won't make you cry," I grin as I gently squeeze Erin's hand. "But I can't promise I won't," I add, then give her a wink.

As Helena and I work together to position Erin, my heart feels like it's about to burst. Overcome by a wave of sensual nostalgia for the young Erin, I return to my position and glance down at the film counter.

Realizing I have only one shot left and want to avoid

interruptions, I quickly fire off the shot and then hand the camera to Mark, who swiftly passes another freshly loaded Rolleiflex.

Helena walks away, and suddenly, my eyes meet my past. I'm overcome with conflicting emotions as I raise the viewfinder to my eye. Gazing at my lovely Erin, I want to burst into tears.

Buying some time, I look at Mark and say, "Will you please take a meter check on Erin? He quickly walks toward her as I gaze down at my camera.

Helena approaches me and asks, "You okay, Laura?"

"Yeah, I just needed a meter check."

"Laura, the light hasn't changed in the last 30 minutes. Honey, it will be okay. That girl loves you; your past is now your future, Laura. You concentrate on that when you look at her through your camera."

"Damn, how do you know me so well, Helena?"

Smiling, she says, "Because I love you, sweetie."

Nodding, I raise my camera as Mark yells out the meter reading. I shake my head at Helena and give her a big smile, and then my eyes shift to my lovely Erin.

"You look stunning, my love," I shout for the whole crew to hear. Erin gives me a tender smile from the past.

Pulling the viewfinder to my eye, I see her, and time stands still. Erin gives me her raw, vulnerable gaze with the hint of attitude that my heart fell for years ago. My head and heart sync as I gaze at Erin. I press the shutter repeatedly as she moves fluidly, just as she used to.

I pull the camera from my face, and her eyes meet mine. Erin gives me a wink and then giggles. My god, how I love this woman. Laughing, I say, "You're amazing, Erin."

As I finish Erin's session, I walk over to her and see her earthy-green eyes smiling at me. Pulling her close, I whisper,

"I saw you, Erin. I saw my *Beautiful Girl,* but mostly, I saw the woman you've become, and I'm so in love with both of you."

She kisses my cheek and whispers, "And I saw you, but more than that, I felt you. You consume me, Laura. You always have."

As nine o'clock approaches, we begin to wrap up and prepare to head back to the Inn. Helena announces to the team that we'll reconvene at Camden Harbor at three o'clock for the next session.

Erin and I ascend the stairway to the mezzanine, our hands intertwined, excitement coursing through every nerve in my body. We reach my room, and as soon as we're inside, she pulls me close, and our bodies ignite with a fierce, intense desire. Every muscle tightens with the overwhelming urge to love, consume, and possess her completely.

Breaking our kiss, Erin says, "I want you so badly, but not now, baby. I feel like someone will knock on our door at any moment."

Holding her tight, I say, "You're right, but my god, I'm on fire for you, Erin."

"I know, Laura. I could orgasm in about fifteen seconds, but that isn't how I want our first time to be. Taking my hand, she asks, "Is that okay, baby?"

Smiling at her, I reply, "Of course, darling. When I looked through my viewfinder, you overwhelmed me. I wanted to toss my camera and grab and devour you, Erin. What a rush it was to gaze at you again."

Laughing, Erin replies, "Yes, it was an amazing rush. Watching your sexy fingers press the shutter as I felt your eyes on me again brought it all back. I felt a flood of erotic yearning that I used to feel, and now it burns even hotter for you, Laura."

Pushing Erin onto the bed, I straddle her, sit on her lap,

and gaze at her. "I'm so in love with you, Erin," Kissing her scar, I say, "Damn, this scar is fucking sexy as hell. You may not think so, but I believe I could orgasm just looking at it."

"Laura!" She exclaims with laughter.

"I'm dead serious. You're a gorgeous woman, Erin Winslow, and this scar only makes you sexier, baby."

"You're too much, Laura," she says as she holds me tightly. We both begin to giggle like schoolgirls as Erin falls backward, pulling me with her.

"Hmmm, I thought we were going to wait?" I ask seductively.

"Oh, we are. I just wanted to get you all wet for me, Miss Lomax."

"Damn, girl. You have grown up, and honey, I'm soaked."

Erin lets out a moaning growl, then grabs me and sits back up, "Damn, woman, I need a cold shower."

Moving to her ear, I whisper, "Come on, kitten, I'll shower you."

"Oh dear god, Laura. I'm going to orgasm in about five seconds if you don't hush."

"Hush, what, my kitten?" I whisper seductively into her ear.

Erin stands us up and says, "We've got to go outside or something, Laura." I see the look on her face and take her hand as I giggle.

"I'm sorry, Erin. My playfulness got away from me, darling. Let's go downstairs and wait for lunch. Okay?"

Nodding, Erin says, "Yes, but Laura, I can't even imagine what it's going to be like making love with you."

Putting my arms around her waist, I gaze into her eyes and say, "It's going to be magical, Erin." She pauses, then tugs at my hand and adds, "Come on, darling, let's have some lunch."

It's 3:30, and the crew and I are at Camden Harbor. I've been photographing the other models since 3:00. Trying to stay focused on the task, I purposely avoid looking at the 'shoot list.' It's easier not knowing when Erin's turn will come.

I'm sure Helena knows this because she has yet to approach me as usual, letting me know who's next. She waits until the model is up, and then we approach her and work on the pose and the aesthetics of the shot.

As Mark hands me a freshly loaded camera, I see Erin, and she takes my breath away. She's wearing a classic Victor Voss Emerald Green Cardigan, a deep, rich shade that complements her perfectly. Her short, thick, golden brown hair frames her face, adding to the sweater's luxurious feel. The deep green plays beautifully against the warmth of her hair, making her look effortlessly stunning.

Approaching Erin, I smile at her and wink, then turn toward Helena. "Laura, we have this cardigan in four colors, so I'm going to get Erin to change it quickly after you shoot each one," Helena says.

Touching Erin's arm, I ask, "Are you okay, darling?"

She gives me a confident nod and wink. My heart flutters, and I feel like I'm gliding as I walk back to my position. Raising the camera, I peer through the viewfinder again at my lovely Erin.

There is that look, the one she only allows me to see. As I press the shutter, Erin and I become one as we work together. Erin needs little direction; she's always been a natural, so attempting to pose her would simply be a waste.

As we work through the shots with her in the cardigans, she slips into the last one—a pastel pink. The gentle color contrasts beautifully with her sharp features and defined jawline, accentuating her elegance. Her short, thick hair frames her face neatly, adding a refined touch to the overall look. It's a striking combination that makes this my favorite cardigan on her.

CHAPTER 10

LAURA

Entering the dining hall, I notice most of the crew gathered around a large table, so I make my way over to join them. As soon as I sit down, Julie asks, "Where's Erin?"

With a smile, I respond, "She's on her way. She wanted to change clothes."

Mark chimes in, "Erin was amazing today, Laura. She saved this shoot, I can tell you that, Honey! And that girl is drop-dead gorgeous, just like I said when we boarded her plane."

Laughing and feeling a bit proud, I simply say, "Yes, she is indeed, Mark."

As Erin enters the dining hall, the entire crew applauds her, and I watch my lovely woman's eyes search for me. When I rise to meet her, she walks to me, and I gaze lovingly into her earthy green eyes before giving her a kiss on the cheek. She looks slightly embarrassed by the crew's praise but says, "Thank you, I'm enjoying this more than you know. I appreciate all of you for being so kind to me."

During dinner, Erin and I exchange tender glances amidst

the lively chatter from the crew. Helena eventually makes her way over and sits beside me. She leans over, looks at Erin, and says, "Honey, you were amazing today. You fit in well with the crew, and we expect you again next year."

Erin glances at me, looking somewhat uneasy. I meet Helena's eyes and say, "Erin has her own aviation company that keeps her busy, so I'm afraid this may be a one-time thing."

Helena replies, "We'll see about that. I have a feeling when this line is out, and the whole world sees how amazing Erin is, she'll be in high demand, Laura."

Turning toward Erin, I wink and ask, "Are you finished, darling?" She nods at me as we rise to retreat to our room. "I hope you all have a good evening. We will see you all at 5am."

After the crew bids us good evening, Erin and I ascend the stairs to our rooms on the mezzanine again. Once inside, I pull Erin close and kiss her tenderly. Her lips are so gentle and soft, just like her heart.

Pulling away, I say, "Everyone loves you, darling." Then I take her hand and add, "Come on, let's sit by the warm fire."

Erin and I settle in comfortably by the warm fire. It pops and crackles as we gaze into the flickering light.

She turns and smiles at me and says, "They're amazing, Laura. I'm enjoying myself, especially when you're photographing me. It feels magical having your eyes on me again as I gaze at you through the camera's lens, showing you my vulnerability. Laura, you're the only woman I've ever allowed to see that side of me.

Whispering intimately, I reply, "I know, darling. It's our sweet connection. Why have you always shown me your raw and vulnerable side, Erin?"

Erin gazes into the constant fire. "Laura, you're my soul-mate. I let you in long ago, and I can't imagine not allowing you to see my vulnerability."

"Yes, we are soulmates, darling," I say tenderly as I hold her warm hand.

"Laura, I have something that I need and want from you."

"Darling, I'll give you the world. Whatever you need from me, I'll give you," I reply softly as I tenderly squeeze her hand.

As she gazes back into the fire, I see she's hesitant, making my heart slightly fearful. "Have I done something wrong, love?"

Turning toward me, she smiles and nods, "No, baby." Then she pauses. I realize she needs me to be patient, so I relax as I gaze at her and wait.

"It's difficult for me to put into words, Laura, but I know it's what I need, and I think you need it too." I nod and continue being patient.

Erin turns toward me and says, "You know before lunch how uncontrolled we were for one another."

With a soft giggle, I say, "It would be hard for me to forget that, darling."

"Laura, after spending the day in front of the camera with you, my thoughts have drifted back to our love from years ago and how you made me feel when we were together. I loved you so much, and I still do, baby. But today, for the past few hours, I've felt like 19-year-old Erin again with you. I can't quite explain it, but it's been overwhelming."

"Erin," I whisper. Gazing back at the fire, I say, "I felt it, too. Gazing at you through my viewfinder, I saw *My Beautiful Girl,* and I fell in love with you all over again." As the fire dances and crackles for us, the room goes silent as we hold hands and peering into the firelight.

Gazing at her, I ask, "What do you need from me, Erin? I'll do anything, darling."

She hesitates for a moment, then softly says, "Laura, I need and want you to make love to nineteen-year old Erin."

As my gaze grows intense, she looks at me and our souls from the past touch.

"I don't feel like I can make love with you at this age until nineteen-year-old Erin has been loved and set free.

Standing, I walk to the door and put the 'Do not disturb' sign on the door, not giving a damn what the others may think. I walk back to Erin and reach for her hand. She looks at me, completely open and vulnerable, longing for the Laura from her past—the one who should have taken her to bed years ago.

Turning off the lamps, I pull her to me, touch her cheek, and bring her to my lips. Whispering on her lips, "I love you, *My beautiful girl.*"

As I undress Erin, I take my time with her, kissing her sweetly as I would have done years ago. Unzipping her slacks, I kneel in front of her, pull them down, and see her black satin panties. Removing her slacks, I leave her panties on, then stand and pull her lips against mine. Kissing her tenderly, just as I would have kissed her years ago.

Noticing that Erin has gotten a bit shy, I whisper, "It's okay, my love. "I'm going to love you so tenderly."

Gazing at Erin, tears pool in her lovely green eyes, so I kiss them away. Stepping back, I quickly undress myself, leaving my eyes on her. She whispers, "My god, you're gorgeous, Laura."

Kneeling back in front of Erin, I lower myself and smell her. Closing my eyes, I'm overcome with a strong desire to take her forcefully. As I gaze up at her, I begin removing her panties slowly and then place my face against her erotic sexual mound that is just waiting to be taken and loved. Threading her fingers through my hair, she looks down at me and whispers, "Yes, Laura."

CHAPTER 11

LAURA

How could I not have known Erin needed this? She's a woman now, so I thought that's where our sexual encounter would begin, but I was so very wrong. Gazing up at her, I search for my 19-year-old Erin; she smiles at me. "I see you," I whisper.

Smiling at me, she closes her eyes and lets me love her. As I stand, I gaze at her and reach around her, slowly unhooking her brassiere. Erin leans into me and sighs, whispering, "Laura, Laura."

Pulling her close, I cradle her gently against my chest and whisper, "Let's get in bed." As I catch a glimpse of Erin's body, my breath falters—the scars that trace her skin tell the painful story of the plane crash and her survival. I quickly avert my eyes, meeting her gaze instead, where innocence and trust shimmer. My heart tightens with devotion as I focus on loving my 19-year-old Erin, just as she asked me.

There will be time to love the scars of my 30-year-old Erin, but now, in my bed, lies the perfect body and soul of the young woman I've loved forever. *My Beautiful Girl* lies next to me, and she needs to be released, and I'm the only one who can set her free.

Moving under the covers, we turn on our sides, facing one another. Touching Erin's face, I whisper, "Close your eyes." After she closes them, I begin, "We are back in the darkroom years ago, bathed in the amber glow of the darkroom light. I look at you sensually, and you come to me and kiss me just as you did. I'm taking you in my arms again, Erin, and loving you just as I did that night. But I'm not pulling away; I continue loving you back and my fire for your burns. As our love grew, you and I shared many intimate glances and nights."

Erin whimpers as I recount the past as it was and how it should have been.

As I continue, I say, "I'm taking you by the hand and leading you upstairs to my bedroom, and I undress you, Erin. I gaze at your lovely body. The same one I've fantasized about forever, the one I've made love to over and over in my dreams, baby. You're in my bed, and it's eleven years ago. Forty-year-old Laura is holding you, and I have loved and craved you for the past year."

Open your eyes, Erin? As she opens her eyes to meet mine I ask, "Who are you right now?"

She whispers, "I'm nineteen-year-old Erin, who's been in love with you for the past two years, Laura."

"Yes, you are, baby. You're my nineteen-year-old beauty, the one I crave, and who's in my bed and aching to make love to, my beautiful girl."

"Oh, Laura, I feel you. We are back in time, and I need you so badly."

"I know you do, Erin, and I need you," I say as I bring her close and kiss her softly. Then, I move on top of her. Gazing down at her, I whisper, "I enjoyed photographing you today, baby. I felt you looking at me. Did you see me, Erin?"

"Yes, Laura, I saw you. I couldn't wait to come home with you and be with you like we do every night."

"I love you here with me in my home, Erin. I'd be lost without you," I whisper softly. Then I move my body between her legs and kiss her neck and then begin moving against her, pushing my sex against hers. Erin puts her arms around me and pulls me into her.

"Your body feels so good against me, Laura." Continuing my tenderness with her, I push against her and feel her needing more. "This is what I've always wanted, Laura. I've longed for you to take me to your bed."

I kiss her soft lips and say, "It's also what I've always desired."

Moving to her full breasts, I gently take them in my hands and gaze up at her. Erin is watching me. I place one of her erect nipples in my mouth and suck it sweetly and gently as I gaze into the eyes I fell in love with years ago. "That feels so incredible, Laura. I knew you would be tender with me."

Sucking her beasts, I feel my erotic lust for her burn and pulse, but it will have to wait. This is nineteen-year-old Erin, who must be loved tenderly and with my whole heart.

Looking back at her, I whisper, "Do you remember the first time we met a year ago, baby?"

"Yes," she whispers breathlessly.

As I continue licking her nipples, I say, "I fell for you then, Erin."

"You did, Laura?"

"Yes, Erin. I remember that photo shoot as if it were yesterday. I whisper softly against her nipples."

"You were so young, but how you looked at me captured my soul, and that's where you've remained, baby."

"Laura, you loved me then?" she asks.

Moving to her tummy, I lick it and confess, "Yes, Erin. I fell for you at that moment. You were wearing a navy sweater that you were modeling, and the late afternoon sun caught your soft locks of hair and turned them golden brown. You glowed, my love."

"Oh, Laura. You've never told me this."

"I know, but I'm telling you now, Erin. That was a year ago. Do you remember that day ?' I ask as I move to her soft feminine mound and smell her again.

"Laura, of course, I remember. My world stopped when I walked out and saw that you were the photographer. I was so nervous."

"Why were you nervous, baby? I ask as Erin parts her legs for me.

Moaning, Erin whispers, "Because you took my breath away. I felt your eyes on me, and you made me feel like I was the only model there."

Pulling Erin's feminine folds tenderly, I whisper against her clit. "You were the only one I saw that day, Erin." Then I begin to lick her swollen clit tenderly. Tasting her sweet fruit that was open for me years ago, but I was too foolish to partake.

"Laura, that feels indescribable. As I continue with my tongue against Erin's swollen clit I hear her say, "I never wanted you to look at any of the models except for me. Did you know that?"

Pushing my tongue in uniform movements back and forth against her clit I think of that moment and know that's when I fell in love with Erin. Yes, I fell in love with her when she was only eighteen, but I could never admit that.

"Why didn't you want me looking at the other girls, Erin?" I ask as I continue loving her clit.

"Because you were mine, Laura."

"Yes, I was, baby. I've always been yours, I whisper onto her clit. Then I continue loving it, pushing my tongue firmly against her swollen clit.

"Laura, I'm so close."

"I know, baby, I feel you. May I go inside you?"

"Yes, please," She moans. As she parts her legs, I enter her leaving my tongue on her clit. I begin to give her tender, gentle thrusts. "Yes, Laura. I've needed this; I craved you."

"I know, baby."

Leaving my fingers deep inside her, I move back to her face, gaze into her earthy-green eye, and smile at her as I continue with soft thrusts. I ask, "Does this feel good, baby?"

"Yes, you have no idea." Kissing her deeply, I begin to increase the pace of my thrust, and Erin responds, "Yes, Laura." She whispers sweetly, "I'm yours."

Gazing down at her, I begin to thrust deeper as I watch her eyes. "I've only ever loved you, Laura," Erin whispers softly, her eyes filled with sincerity and warmth as she holds my gaze.

"And you're all I've loved since the first day I met you, Erin," I tell her as I gaze into her eyes.

Watching her desire grow, I whisper, "Yes, baby. Open for me."

Erin whimpers and moans deeper as I keep the same thrust and pace. Moving on top of her, I pull out gently and gather her liquid and move my fingers to her clit. As I gaze into her soul, I press firmly against her, making uniform circles. Erin is laying bare her vulnerability for me as I push against her clit. I ask her, "Will you come for me, *My Beautiful Girl*?

She whimpers, "Yes, Laura."

"Why me, Laura?" She asks as I press harder onto her clit.

"Why do you think, Erin?"

"I don't know, Laura. Please tell me." She pleads with me as I press harder and faster on her swollen clit.

With her heart laid bare, I press harder, and our souls

touch. She is ready to come but needs me to explain why I fell for her.

Pressing harder and faster, I say, "The moment I saw you, my world lit up, and from that first glance, Erin, I fell completely and instantly in love with you."

Erin threads her fingers through my hair and then cries out as she looks into my eyes and soul, "Laura, I'm coming for you." Keeping my fingers taut against her clit I watch her fall back in time. I watch and feel this tender girl from my past orgasm for me, just as she has done hundreds of times in my fantasies.

As It ends, I look at her and say, "Come again for me, Erin." Then I press firmer and faster and watch her fall again and again, giving her every orgasm I can, wanting to somehow make up for the ones I should have given her years ago.

Again, she whispers, "I'm coming, Laura." I wrap my arms around her, hold her to me, and kiss her tenderly. Then I hear, "I love you, Laura. Please never leave me again."

Searching her face, I suddenly see my thirty-year-old Erin come back to me, and my blood runs hot; I enter her and then begin thrusting fast and hard. I just loved *My Beautiful Girl* and released her. Now, lying in my bed is my passionate 30-year-old woman, and I feel an overwhelming need to possess her completely.

As our eyes meet, I see the woman who flew me to Maine, and I grin at her with a sensual eagerness. She grabs my face, looks into my eyes, and says, "Take me, Laura. Take me so hard, baby."

An erotic rush comes coursing through my feminine region as I gaze at this woman with the sexy scar that makes my pussy ache with indescribable pain. "Yes, I'll take you, darling. Like this?" I ask as I unleash a powerful thrust up inside her.

"Harder, Laura, I know you have more." Grinning at her, I give her the rest of the strength held back as I make love to young Erin.

"How about this, darling? I ask as I fuck her intensely.

"Yes, that's more like it. Don't you stop until I tell you," Erin says vehemently.

Grinning, I do as I'm told and keep thrusting hard and fast, releasing my passion into her. "Yes, Laura. Look at me," she demands.

Gazing at her, I see a completely different woman than I took to my bed an hour ago. This is the woman of my future. The girl I loved dearly has been released and has grown into the passionate woman I crave. "Come for me, Erin. You come for me now," darling.

Erin threads her fingers through my hair as before, but this time, she grabs my locks of hair and holds onto me with fury as she lets out a whaling moan, "Yes, I'm coming so hard, Laura. Don't stop!" She demands.

Again, I grin, knowing this woman was worth the wait. She is incredible and every bit the woman I need and desire."

I get on my knees and pull Erin up with me. I grab her and pull her tightly against my body, then thrust up inside her harder and faster, "Come again for me, Erin." I demand.

Closing her eyes, she has an intense look on her face. Then it begins to soften as I feel her beginning to orgasm, "Come for me, baby. Yes, come all over me, darling."

Erin moans and her body grows weak, but I hold her firmly as she orgasms. Then I move back to her clit and press against it, moving against it with hard and fast circles. Erin opens her eyes but doesn't speak. I watch her fall again, and I wink at her. Her expression is almost blank because she is so depleted, but she comes again for me as I whisper, "Yes, come once more, darling." I say as I keep pressure against her clit, and I see tears in her eyes, but I hold her tightly and don't release her.

"I'm not releasing you until you come once more," I say with conviction. With that, Erin lets out a faint and exhausted moan as she orgasms one last time.

Hugging her weak body, I cradle her gently against the bed. As I lie on top of her, my arms encircle her, pulling her close. My breath brushes her ear as I whisper, "Erin, I'm so in love with you. You'll never slip away from me again, do you understand?"

She nods, her voice barely a whisper. "Yes, Laura." I hold her even tighter, feeling her warmth against me. "Erin, you're my everything, darling. I never want to face another day on this earth without you." Tears slip from my eyes as I press her close, my soul both weeping and rejoicing in this quiet, intimate moment.

CHAPTER 12

ERIN

I wake to the steady rhythm of my lover's heartbeat, perfectly in tune with the flickering flames from the fire, casting a warm glow across our room. Turning my head toward Laura, I place my face into her soft, dark hair and inhale the same aroma I smelled as she tenderly loved me.

I want to jump up and scream to celebrate our love, but I lie quietly and let her sleep. Laura had a long day of shooting, and then she made love to me for hours, so I'll let her stay in her sweet dreams for now.

Gazing into the fire, I see it blazing. Laura must have placed another log on it not long ago. I wonder if she kissed my lips and gazed at me when she crawled in beside me. I grin, imagining that she did. Continuing to smell her, I replay our lovemaking, and it simply makes me smile.

Lying next to Laura, I search my heart for the young Erin, but she isn't there. I realize she's finally free and fulfilled now that her one true love, Laura, made love to her so tenderly— just as she had longed for all those years ago.

Smiling, I snuggle close to Laura and drift off as I inhale her once more before surrendering to midnight's embrace.

"Good Morning, my sexy woman," I hear Laura whisper. Pulling her to me, I giggle, then crawl on top of her and kiss her deeply.

"My god, Laura, you were incredible last night, and I am burning with a painful lust for you right this minute."

As Laura laughs, I push her body against the bed and gaze down at her, "You are so lovely, Laura."

"It's 4:15, darling, I'm afraid it will have to wait."

"Oh hell!" I exclaim.

Rising, I put another log on the fire as Laura sits on the edge of the bed waiting for me. I walk back to her, kneel before her, and say, "Well, I have a special place. I want to make love to you anyway, so it's just as well."

Laura smiles as she searches my face, "Where?" She asks.

"That's a secret," I say as she giggles and nods.

"Erin, will you stand for me, baby?"

Knowing why she wants me to stand, I find some bravery and rise as she asks, "I know you saw them last night, but you may look at me, Laura." Standing close she gazes at each and every one of my numerous scars with her loving eyes.

"Yes, I saw them, darling. But I want to know about each of them," she says tenderly as she touches them.

Pulling her close, I softly reply, "I'll tell you everything, Laura."

Nodding, she gets close to my lips and whispers, "I need to shower quickly. Are you coming down for breakfast?"

Grinning at her, I tease, "After the way you made love to me last night, I don't think I can stand to be more than two feet away from you."

Laura laughs loudly and says, "Good, let's shower together."

"Yes, ma'am!" I say firmly as I grab her and pull her to the bathroom."

"Oh, goodness. Someone's in a good mood this morning."

As the warm water cascades over us, I begin lathering up her sexy, mature body that will be mine today. I pull her to me and whisper, "I'm going to love every inch of this 51-year-old voluptuous body of yours today, Miss Lomax."

"Erin! Honey, I have got to keep my head on straight!" Laughing at her, I step back and watch her continue bathing. I simply grin at her. With a smile, she asks, "What's this special place you're taking me to?"

"Oh, you will have to wait and see," I say as I step out and begin drying off. Laura steps out of the shower, still grinning. I open a fresh towel for her, and she walks into it. Then, I wrap it around her gorgeous body. Grinning, I say, "I'm not scheduled to be photographed this morning, so I'll pick you up at 9:00 in a taxi. Bring your camera and a roll of high-speed black-and-white film."

As she dries off she looks puzzled but simply says, "Okay, but you're being very mysterious, Erin."

Towel drying my hair, I ask, "Is it making you wet?"

Giggling, she says, "Yes, it actually is; you are a sexy vixen."

Pulling her close, I whisper, "Well, I'll take care of that today, baby." Then I pull away and gaze at her and add, "By the way, be prepared for me to fuck you as well as you fucked me last night before you put me in a coma."

"Erin! My gosh! What has gotten into you!?"

"Laura Lomax, I whisper in her ear," Then I dash to the bedroom to dress for breakfast as I continue laughing.

She walks into the bedroom, still drying off, with the

same grin. Then she pulls me close and says, "You're different, Erin."

Touching her face, I reply, "You were so tender with young Erin last night, Laura, but when you released her, I saw you in a different light. My erotic soul burned for you, Laura, and I didn't know if I wanted to consume you, or be consumed."

"It *was* pretty awesome, Erin." She exclaims.

"That's the first time I've made love to two women in the same night."

"And it will be your last, Miss Lomax!"

Laura laughs loudly, then says, 'Put your cardigan on, sexy, and let's head down for breakfast. And yes, pick me up at 9:00 this morning back at the Harbor." Then her breath brushes my ear as she whispers, "I don't know what you have planned today, but it better include giving me multiple orgasms, darling."

• Holding my hand out for hers, I wink and say, "That's only part of it, love."

"Damn!" Laura says with a chuckle.

As we walk to the door, I give Laura's ass a playful swat. She glances over her shoulder at me, blushes, and then laughs.

9:00 am Camden Harbor

Leaning against the taxi, I watch Laura continuing the shoot. As I reflect on last night and the erotic voyage she took me on, I can't help but think, *"My god, had I known she was this amazing in bed, I'd have sought her out years ago,"* then I chuckle to myself.

As everyone wraps up for the morning, I see Laura's eyes searching for me. She sees me and gives me a grin. Handing her camera to Mark, I see her reach down and grab another Rollieflex and a roll of film just as I ask.

Approaching me, our eyes meet, and our unspoken love is almost overwhelming. "Hello, my love," I say softly, then greet her with a kiss on her cheek.

Laura kisses me back and says, "Good Morning again, darling. Where are you taking me?"

I smile and say, "You'll see." Then I give her a tender wink.

As the taxi pulls up to my plane I then instruct him to pick us up at 1 o'clock. Taking Laura's hand, I help her up the boarding steps. I close them, then hop in through the pilot's door and immediately see Laura sitting in the seat beside me.

"Erin, you are so utterly charming. Why have you continued to love me for so long?"

Smiling at her as I start the engine, I reply, "Because you're my soulmate, Laura."

She reaches for my hand, and our fingers instantly intertwine, finding their familiar and loving places.

As we ascend, I hold Laura's hand tight and say, "I'm taking you on a short sightseeing excursion."

"Oh, Erin. This is magical, darling. Look, Erin! I see the Harbour where we've spent much of our time shooting," she says excitingly.

"Are you happy?" I ask.

Laura turns her head toward me and whispers through the microphone, "Happier than I've been in forever, Erin." Smiling at her, I kiss her hand.

"Over there is the Curtis Island Lighthouse. I wanted us to fly along the coast and see the Harbors."

"This is magnificent, Erin. Seeing the Atlantic Ocean meeting the shoreline, docks, and harbors." Smiling, I watch the scenery, but I mainly look at my lovely Laura and see her happiness.

"I'm going to circle back now. This was only part of the

day I have planned with you." Laura looks at me and searches my face with a grin. "Hmmm," she utters through the microphone. I giggle at her.

Laura grips my hand tightly as we descend and asks, "Where is this, Erin? This isn't the same airport we flew out of."

Grinning at her, I wink and say, "No, this one is more private."

Staring at me as she fights back a grin, she shakes her head and tightens the grip on my hand. After we land, I taxi to a secluded area away from the airport. Then I shut off the engine. "You've got me incredibly nervous, darling."

"Baby, there's no need for you to be nervous. I've already asked the landowner for permission to stay here for a couple of hours. I told him I needed to rest in my plane for a while."

"Rest, huh?" She asks amusingly.

"Yes, and every door is locked and secured, so please relax and trust me, love." She nods with a smile as she touches my cheek.

As I slide out of my pilot seat, I stand and help Laura out of her seat, then ask her to sit in one of the club chairs. She sits and spins around to watch me as I convert the couch into a bed. I pull out a couple of pillows and two blankets from storage, then grab two glasses, an ice bucket, and a bottle of champagne from the side compartment.

Glancing at Laura, she looks completely amazed. "Erin, when did you plan all of this?"

"Most of it was planned as I held you in my arms this morning and listened to your heartbeat in rhythm with the warm firelight. Then, after breakfast, I took care of the logistics and the champagne."

As I fold the bedding, I feel Laura encircle me from behind. I turn to her and see her eyes glisten. Touching her face, I whisper, "I love you, Laura, and I always have."

Closing her eyes, she touches my hand and kisses it, then opens her eyes to greet my love. I whisper, "I know it's early, but would you like some champagne?"

"Yes, darling, please," She says sweetly as she sits on the bed.

After popping the top of the champagne, I pour each of us a small glass, sit beside her, and ask, "What would you like to toast to, Laura?"

"Well, I don't know, darling, but it should be very special," she says softly. Then she adds, "Erin, I want to toast to *My Beautiful Girl. Is* that okay? She is free now, so I feel as though we should toast to her happiness."

"That makes me happy, Laura. You should make the toast then."

Laura looks deeply into me and whispers sweetly, "To *My Beautiful Girl,* the lovely girl who brought me so much love and happiness, as well as this amazing woman who sits beside me."

With tears in our eyes, we touch glasses in a toast to the young girl somewhere beyond our reach but safe. Then we sit gazing at one another as we sip our champagne.

Setting our empty champagne glasses down, I look at Laura and smile. "God, you're such a gorgeous woman, Laura. You stole my heart years ago," I whisper softly as I unbutton her sweater.

Laura reaches for me and begins unbuttoning my blouse as we kiss. I feel my lust rising, and my heart pounds and aches. As I continue to undress her slowly, I kiss Laura deeply; her tongue is warm, and I feel it begin to fight for me.

CHAPTER 13

LAURA

Erin continues to undress me slowly, and I feel myself beginning to burn for her. I feel my wetness, which is accompanied by a throbbing pain, and my desire to be taken. I brush my breath against her ear and say, "Take me, Erin."

Erin stands and immediately undresses, then pulls me up toward her. She brushes against my cheeks as she slowly unzips my slacks. I let out a moaning whisper, "Oh, god, Erin."

Lowering herself, she gazes up at me, removes my slacks, and then lays them on one of the club chairs. She slowly pulls down my panties. Her eyes drift away from mine as she looks at my feminine mound. She lays her face against it as she removes my panties.

Erin turns her head upward and meets my gaze, then leans into my feminine essence and inhales me as her earthy green closes. She takes several breaths of me, then reaches around and grabs my ass, pulling me against her face and continuing to breathe me. Threading my fingers through her soft brown locks, I watch Erin inhale my scent.

She stands, then removes my brassier and looks at my breast. "I only got to gaze at your bosoms last night and in the shower this morning, but now I wish to consume them," She whispers across my lips.

Erin sits on the bed and asks me to straddle her. I crawl willingly onto her lap and let her hold me. "Laura, I've waited so long for you," she says softly.

I brush against her ear and whisper, "So have I, darling."

Erin grabs me with incredible strength as she gazes into my eyes, pulls my lips to hers, and then gives me an emotionally charged kiss full of tender passion. As our kisses grow, Erin grips me tighter, grasping my hair with one hand and my ass with the other. My feminine soul pulses with wet pain, and my heart aches with love.

Erin is so tenderly alluring as she pulls me tight and then lies back as I remain sitting on top of her. We catch hands, and she gazes at my breasts, her eyes fixed on them as I see those earthy-green gems begin to grow seductive.

She moves back up and grabs me again, kissing me forcefully, her tongue twirls rhythmically around mine, and then she delicately sucks my tongue into her mouth and begins feeding on it tenderly. I start to lose my breath as she continues loving my tongue. She moves her hands to my breasts and brushes the back of her fingertips against my nipples. They immediately peak, and then she gently holds them as she releases my tongue.

Erin gazes at my breasts, holds them, and then she pushes her face into them. Gripping the back of her hair, I pull her away just enough so she can see them again. Erin's eyes meet mine, then she winks at me, taking one of my nipples into her mouth. She sucks it softly, I want more, but she isn't in any hurry, so I let her take me however she wishes.

"I want to devour you, Laura," she says as she begins

sucking my nipples harder. Then adds, "I want you tenderly as well as forcefully."

She looks at me sincerely and asks, "Which do you desire right now, Laura?"

"Both!" I reply as we giggle.

"You're amazing, Erin. You take me as you wish, darling," she says sweetly. Erin pulls away again, searching my eyes to read my desire.

She immediately pulls me to the bed, stretches her whole body out, easing it onto mine, and grins at me. Placing my arms around her, I pull her close, and instantly, we're lost in a heated, intense kiss. Erin's tongue pushes forcefully against mine as her hands grip my face. I whisper against her lips, "Yes, Erin."

She pulls away and looks into my eyes again, then moves her hand between my legs, finding my warm, soaked sex. She touches me as she gazes into my soul, gathers my wetness, and then moves to my clit, making back-and-forth movements.

Her touch isn't simply to initiate an orgasm; it's to let me know that she's aware of my needs. "Yes, my lovely Laura," she says sweetly against my lips.

Erin moves on top of me and then between my legs that I've opened for her. She pushes against me firmly, never releasing my eyes. I thread my hands through her soft hair, enjoying her love. She pushes harder against me, then lowers her mouth to my bosoms and begins loving them. Holding them together, she sucks each one tenderly, then begins pulling them harder as she sucks and continues pushing her sex against mine.

Releasing them, she looks me in the eyes and says, "I smelled you on me all night, and I've waited years to taste you, Laura. I won't wait another minute."

Erin slips off the bed onto her knees and pulls me to her. I open my legs, and she leans in to smell me. "Laura," she whispers against my sex. Then adds, "Your aroma is so intoxicating, I could orgasm just from inhaling you."

I smile, then feel Erin massage the inside of my thighs and see her staring at my feminine essence. She licks the inside of my thighs and makes her way slowly to my overpowering ache. She is within inches of my clit, and I feel her smelling me again. "Erin," I whisper.

She glances at me and asks, "What do you want, Laura?"

"I want you to take me...You know exactly what I want, baby."

"I do, but I wanted to hear it from your pretty lips." Erin places her whole mouth on my pussy and then moves across my clit with her entire tongue."

"Oh, Erin... honey."

"You taste like the deep dark ocean at midnight, Laura," She whispers on my clit. Then, begins loving me again. I thread my fingers through her hair and pull her against my painful wetness.

Erin's love for me is almost overwhelming. I released young Erin last night but also feel an overwhelming desire to release the younger Laura.

Sitting up, I pull her to me and then look at her as I touch her face and smile. "What do you need, Laura?"

As I begin to weep, Erin holds me close. "It's okay, talk to me."

Pulling back, I gaze into her sweet eyes and softly say, "The younger Laura needs releasing, too; she should be with her, *"Beautiful Girl."*

Gazing deeply into my eyes, I see Erin's eyes glisten, and she nods. She then pushes me back tenderly against the bed and begins to love my clit softly, just as young Erin would have. As I weep, I close my eyes and see *My Beautiful Girl* smiling at me on a bright and beautiful beach. She begins to walk toward me. She's gliding across the brilliant sands of time, giving me that sweet smile from years ago. I start to laugh as she gets close to me.

As Erin continues her tender movements against my clit I feel myself peaking. Young Erin embraces me on our brilliant beach. I gaze at her and softly say, *"I love you, baby, and I have since I met you."*

Young Erin pulls me to the sand, lies beside me, and whispers, "Let me hold you, Laura." As we embrace, I begin to orgasm.

As young Erin holds me against her warm body, I whisper, "Yes, baby, hold me." She pulls me tight and whispers, "Let go, Laura. Then you can be free with me."

With that, I begin to climax as I hold young Erin, who is gazing into my eyes. I see her love for me, and I let go. "I'm coming, *My Beautiful Girl.*"

Pulling me tighter, she softly says, *"I love you, Laura."* My orgasm is intense and emotionally draining as young Erin watches me fall. She kisses me deeply and holds me with more strength than I ever knew she had.

"Laura, I feel you, baby." As the orgasm ends, I gaze into Erin's earthy eyes and see her youth and her love for me.

She stands and reaches for my hand. I gaze up at her, smiling as I stand beside her. Pulling me close, she says, "I've been waiting for you, Laura." She gives me that vulnerable smile I know so well. "Come with me, Laura. You and I will never be separated again."

Taking her hand, I smile and wink at her. She giggles, and together, we walk up the coastline into the magnificent, radiant light that embraces and consumes us.

Opening my eyes, I see my grown 30-year-old Erin and

smile at her. She moves on top of me, threads her fingers through my hair, and softly asks, "Are they together?"

Nodding with tears, I say, "Yes, they walked up a magnificent and brilliant shoreline together, hand in hand, darling."

Erin looks at me, startled. Touching her face, I ask, "What's wrong, my love?" She smiles and kisses me softly.

"That was the dream I had as my plane crashed. You and I were on a bright coastline, and I was playing in the sand. You asked, "What are you doing, *My Beautiful Girl?*"

Moving back onto Erin's lap, I pull her against me, "My god, Erin, that's unreal." I feel her nodding, so I pull her tight and love her.

Erin pulls away and says, "I'm glad they're together; now they can love one another throughout eternity."

"Yes, they can, Erin."

Erin begins rubbing my ass, and I feel her strength, and I crave her. I grasp a few strands of her hair, pull her to me, and kiss her deeply as my feminine soul burns. "Please fuck me, Erin," I say breathlessly.

She finds my wetness, then enters me pushing deep inside as she gazes into my soul, "I'll fuck you, Laura. My core is on fire for you."

Suddenly, Erin grasps me tightly as she thrusts upward, giving me every ounce of her loving strength. "Like this, Laura?" She says as she pants.

"Oh, yes, Erin. Just like this, darling." As she continues thrusting upward, she gently lays me back on the bed and then moves on top of me. As she gazes down at me, she begins thrusting again. I pull my legs apart for her and let her take all she needs. "Yes, Erin, just like that. Don't stop."

Erin kisses me deeply as she continues fucking me with impressive strength. Our tongues push against one another. This time I take her tongue and suck it sweetly. Erin gives me a whimpering moan as I hold her tongue as she continues thrusting deep into me. I feel myself tightening around her fingers, so I release her tongue.

She moves to my cheek, and her breath gently whispers, "Come for me, gorgeous." Grasping her face, I gaze at her, and she whispers again, "I said, come for me." With that, I let out a low moan as I close my eyes and rest my head against her shoulder.

"I'm coming, Erin. Please don't stop."

"I won't stop, Laura. Just keep coming, love." As Erin continues with the same pace and thrust, I orgasm again, holding onto her.

"Erin," I whisper to her." Pulling out gently, she moves to my clit, pressing hard against it, and then pulls back to gaze into my eyes. I catch her gaze, seize her earthy-green eyes, and feel myself falling again. Erin gives me orgasm after orgasm, never releasing my eyes.

"Yes, baby. I love you, Laura," she says softly. Then she moves on top of me and enters again. With one of my nipples in her mouth, she thrusts upward, letting me feel her love and strength. We are in a perfect rhythm.

"Oh god, Erin, darling. What are you doing?" She asks as I continue forcefully loving her as promised. Then I hear her let go again; it's a moaning gasp. Releasing her breast from my mouth, I look at her and see Laura is weak and exhausted.

Remembering how she loved me last night, I pull her to her knees and grin, then say, "Come one last time for me, and I'll release you." Laura grins and closes her eyes as my fingers push firmly against her clit and softly say, "Let your sweet pussy come for me, Laura."

She opens her eyes in surprise at my words, grins, and breathlessly whispers, "Yes, I'm coming, darling." She gives me a weak gasp, then looks at me and whispers, "Get me off again, Erin."

Grabbing her from behind, I reach around her and gather more of her overflowing liquid, then bring it back to her clit. "I'll make you come all morning, gorgeous," She says as she holds me tight, pushing against my clit fast and firm. "Oh, Erin," I cry out.

CHAPTER 14

ERIN

As I hold Laura from behind after an intense orgasm, we begin to giggle and fall onto the bed, laughing. "You're a beast, Erin Winslow. My god, woman, you've wrecked me."

Pulling her to me, I softly say, "Who says I'm finished with you, Miss Lomax." Laura giggles and tries to pull away, but I hold her tightly. She begins laughing again.

"You're never getting away from me again, Laura," I say sternly. As we lay spooning, Laura turns her head to me slightly and sighs.

"Who says I want to, Erin. I'd be a fool to let you slip away from me again." Laura wiggles loose, then turns toward me and touches my face and lips. She traces the outline of my lips as she gazes at them. "That was fucking amazing."

Smiling, I nod and kiss her lips tenderly. Laura leans back against the bed, staring at the ceiling, then giggles. "This is the first time I've ever made love in an airplane," she says.

Laughing, I reply, "Me too, but I promise it won't be our last." Laura sits up, then straddles me as I lie beneath her, gazing at her in awe. With fingers intertwined, I say, "You're so beautiful, Laura. Stay with me forever."

She looks down at me with a soft smile and replies, "I'll never let you go or leave you, Erin. You're my beautiful young woman, unbridled and raw, darling. I have no desire to ever set you free."

Pulling her gently to me, I kiss her sweet lips and hold her tenderly. "I should get us back. We both want to return to our room and clean up before lunch."

Laura gazes into my eyes and says, "Can we continue this tonight by the fire?"

Touching her cheek, I reply, "Yes, this was just a warm-up, baby."

"Oh dear lord, Erin. Honey, you have to remember I'm 20 years older," she chuckles.

Rising with her in my arms, I say, "Laura, you were an animal in bed last night. Don't play that age game with me!"

Laura stands and chuckles, then asks, "What were the film and camera for?"

"Oh, I wanted to take pornographic pictures of you," I say as I fall against the bed and laugh. Laura swats my ass.

"Erin! Are you serious?"

Laughing, I say, "No, baby." As I rise, I add, "Well, time got away from us." Laura begins dressing but continues looking at me for an answer.

Then, seriously, I say, "No, baby. I wanted you to take nude photos of me—scars and all—showing my raw vulnerability that you seem to love so much."

"Oh, Erin," she whispers, pulling me to her and hugging me tenderly. Baby, I would love that." She steps away from me and says, "Turn around, Erin." I do as she asks and let her view the long, jagged scar that traces the entire length of my back.

After a moment, I feel her warm, tender lips kissing my

scar. Tenderly, she kisses the marks of the trauma I suffered years ago. The whole length of my back, she kisses every inch of my long scar. Then she encircles me from behind and holds me to her warm body. "You make me so happy, Erin. And you're even more beautiful than you were at nineteen, darling."

As I dress, I ask, "Do you really feel this way, Laura?"

Threading her fingers through my hair, she says, "Erin, I wouldn't say it if it wasn't true. Yes, you've matured into a gorgeous woman, darling. Even Helena's fawning all over you," she chuckles.

As we dress I glance at my watch and see it's 12:15. "We're okay on time, Laura, "I told the taxi guy to pick us up at 1 o'clock. We'll be there in about fifteen minutes. That will give me enough time to tie down the plane and for us to make it back to the Inn for lunch.

Laura pulls me close and says, "Thank you, darling. This was beautiful. You're such a romantic, and this was truly touching. I love you with all my heart."

"I love you, Laura. You're my woman; don't you ever forget that," I say as I wink at her. "Are you ready to head back?"

"No, but we have little choice," she chuckles.

Later that Evening

As Laura and I shower under the cascading warm water, we hug each other and smile. "Erin, today was heavenly. You spoiled me, and now I expect magical excursions like that very often, darling," she says with a playful grin.

"Yes, it truly was heavenly, and I'll take you on another magical excursion whenever you want, baby."

Stepping out of the tub, I find Laura waiting with an open

towel. She wraps it around my body, grinning as she kisses me softly. I whisper against her cheek, "Let's go to bed."

Taking my hand, she leads me to her room, but I stop her. She looks back at me, confused. "Tonight, you're in *my* bed, Miss Lomax."

Laughing, she replies, "Well, okay, Miss Winslow. And will your bed always be open for me?"

With our fingers intertwined, I take her into my warm room, pulling her close to the blazing, crackling fire. "Yes, Laura, my bed will always be open to you, my love," I say softly, then kiss her.

Laura wraps her arms around me, and I hold her tight, feeling her damp body begin to warm by the fire. She softly says, "Please sit, Erin." I sit in the chair beside her, and after a quiet moment, she speaks. "I think we have an issue that needs to be resolved."

Looking at her, slightly confused, I ask, "What is it, Laura?" My heart pounds, unsure of what she means.

"Come here, Erin, please," she says, grinning.

Rising, I then sit on her lap with a playful smile on my face. "What's this issue, Laura?"

"Well, I said my bed will always be open to you, right?" I nod, and she continues, "And now, you say your bed is open to me."

"Of course it is Laura," I say, threading my fingers through her hair.

"Erin, let me hold you for a minute. Let's think about this, okay?"

Leaning into her, I inhale her sweet fragrance, feeling the warmth of her body holding me tight. "It's hard to think when I'm practically burning with lust sitting on your lap, Laura," I tease playfully.

Laughing, she says, "I agree, but look at me, Erin."

As I gaze into her dark eyes, the realization hits me, and I smile. Laughing softly, I wipe away a tear and say, "Are you suggesting we should only have *our* bed?

Touching my cheek, she replies, "That's exactly what I'm saying, Erin."

"How, Laura? I have my place, and you have your home."

"Oh, my sweet Erin, you are my home. From now on, whatever bed we share will be *our* bed. But I'm also asking if you'll live with me, darling. I'll sell my house if it's too painful for you to return to. Maybe you could also consider selling yours, and together, we'll have one home and one bed —forever."

"Laura! I don't know what to say." I sit, gazing into the fire as images of the beautiful life we'll share flash, just as I've always dreamed. They play out vividly in my mind, filling me with hope and longing.

Nodding, I turn back to Laura and say, "We deserve to be together forever, just as *young Erin and Laura* are now. So yes, my love—one home, one bed, throughout eternity."

EPILOGUE ONE

LAURA

Wilmington Island Georgia
September 1949

As I sit on the private pier of the home Erin and I purchased last month on Wilmington Island, I wait for her to return for the evening. The warm afternoon sun kisses my skin as I sip iced tea, my heart anticipating the return of my lovely woman.

After returning home from Camden last spring, Erin and I were thrilled but somewhat overwhelmed by the many decisions ahead of us. We thought of making my house *our* home, but the moment Erin stepped through the front doors, she broke down, weeping uncontrollably.

Without hesitation, I took her in my arms, packed my things, and moved into her home until both houses were sold. Now, here we are—starting a new life full of joy and love that has been constant and will always remain.

Glancing back toward our Colonial Revival Low country

home, I see my lovely Erin approaching me with a bottle of champagne and glasses. Rising, I wait for her so I can continue watching her sexy walk. She still walks like she is gliding elegantly down a fashion runway. "I've been waiting on you, darling," I say with open arms.

Walking to me, she picks me up at my hips and spins me around. She laughs at me while gazing into my eyes. Clutching her brown hair, I say, "Put me down, Erin. What will the neighbors think?"

As she eases me down with that charming grin, she hands me the bottle of wine and sets the glasses on a side table. Then, placing her hands on each side of her mouth, she shouts, "Hey neighbors, just in case you're wondering, I love Laura Lomax with every heartbeat I'm given!"

Covering my mouth, I say, "Oh good heaven, Erin, you didn't just scream that out!" Then I place my hands over my face and shake my head.

"Would you like some champagne to celebrate my public declaration of love for you, Miss Lomax?"

"Oh dear god, Erin. Give me that corkscrew!" I say frantically, grinning, then I begin to laugh loudly. Wrapping my arms around her shoulders, I add, "My soul loves you with every heartbeat I take as well, Erin. I'm so in love with you, and I have been since the first moment I saw you in that navy sweater you were modeling, darling."

Erin pulls me tightly into her embrace and whispers, "When I walked into that room, my world stopped. I thought, *'This is the most beautiful woman I have ever seen.'* And now, Laura, you're mine."

As we sit in our Adirondack chairs on the pier, basking in the evening sun and gazing at the water, I pour each of us a glass of champagne and ask, "What shall we toast to, darling?"

"Is it my turn to make the toast?" Erin asks with a playful grin.

As Laura smiles at me and nods, I search for the perfect words for our toast. Clinking my glass with hers, I say, "Let's toast to our hearts and souls, reunited where they've always belonged, my love."

"That's beautiful, Erin," I say, my eyes glistening. I reach for her hand, and as our fingers intertwine, I'm reminded of the flight to Camden when I first held her hand again after eleven years apart. It felt so different after all those years, yet now, in this moment, it feels so familiar and loving once again.

EPILOGUE TWO

LAURA

The Savannah Grand Hotel
November 1949

As I walk into the lounge of the Savannah Grand Hotel, I immediately see my beautiful friend Helena, looking glamorous as usual. Standing to greet me, she opens her arms and says, "Laura, it's so good to see you! Where's Erin?"

With a chuckle, I say, "Now, Helena, I thought you flew here to see me."

"Oh honey, I did! But any chance I get to feast my eyes on that gorgeous goddess of yours, I will take it! She is so adorable, Laura, and she saved our asses in Camden this past spring."

"That she did, Helena," I reply as I grin with pride. "It's so good to see you, honey. And Erin had to fly some businessmen to Atlanta today, but she'll be at the airport in about an hour."

"Well, I guess I'll just have to cry in my drink," Helena teases.

"You never change, Helena," I say as I shake my head and add, "Congratulations, by the way. My gosh, you are now the Chief Creative Officer of Victor Voss, and I'm not the least bit surprised. You're a powerhouse, and you should have been the CCO a long time ago."

"Thank you, Laura, but these things take time. I've always been perfectly happy as the art director, but when they offered me this position a couple of months back, there was no way I could turn it down."

"You're going to be amazing, Helena, and I'm especially touched that you want to make Lomax Inc. your exclusive fashion photography firm for the whole line of clothing. It's going to be a big job for us. When you have me all booked up, I'll likely have to hire another photographer, maybe two, to accommodate my other clientele."

"Well, I intend to keep you busy because you and I have fun together and always work seamlessly. You'll like the new art director, but if you have any issues, my phone is always open to you 24/7, Laura."

"I appreciate that, Helena. I'm somewhat hesitant about this contract. You and I never had one when I photographed the fall and winter clothing line, but things change, and we have to change with it.

"Unfortunately, we do. The higher-ups couldn't believe you, and I have been doing this for years on a handshake. They glanced at me a bit sideways, but I looked them squarely in the eyes and said, 'Laura Lomax is the best fashion photographer out there, and I wasn't going to insult her with a silly contract.'"

Laughing, I say, "Helena, you didn't say that?"

"I most certainly did. Now that it's the exclusive line for

Victor Voss and I showed my hand, the brass insists on us having a contract. So here it is, honey, and I hate it."

"Well, Helena, a contract isn't going to interfere with our friendship or how we work together."

"You're right about that, Laura, But honey, please look this over carefully before you sign it. Then, when you do, we'll order you a glass of wine, but not before."

Shaking my head with a smile, I begin reading the contract. Everything seems perfectly acceptable and benefits both of us. Just as I'm about to ask for a pen and some wine, a stunning woman with soft, dark eyes that sparkle and shoulder-length raven hair approaches our table. She looks to be around 30, and her presence is immediately captivating.

As I glance up, she is smiling at Helena, so I glance back at the contract and reread it to give them a moment. However, I can't help but overhear them.

"Hi Helena, You may not remember me, but I'm Alex Carrington, and I was one of your models years ago." I can't help but glance up and watch their interaction.

"Alex!" she exclaims as she rises. Of course, I remember you, Alex," she says with a charming smile—one that I've never seen Helena give anyone. It makes me grin. Then she gives Alex a kiss on the cheek, and Alex immediately hugs her closely and gives her a much more extended kiss.

Still smiling at Alex, Helena pulls away, looks at me, and says, "Alex, this is Laura Lomax of Lomax Inc."

"The fashion photographer?" she says delightfully.

As I extend my hand to greet this beautiful woman, I say, "Yes, I'm Laura, and it's so nice to meet you, Alex. You're very beautiful. Are you still modeling?"

She looks uncomfortable and then says, "No, not really," before her sparkling eyes return to Helena. Suddenly, I feel like a third wheel amid an undeniable connection.

I interrupt quickly and say, "Helena, why don't you and I

have breakfast or lunch tomorrow to go over this contract," I say as I push it back to her, then add, "I need to get to the airport, Erin will be there soon, and we have plans. Is that okay?"

"Helena looks into my eyes, and we immediately know each other's thoughts. I give her a playful grin and then stand to leave."

As I rise, Helena stands and says, "Alex, please have a seat. I'll be right back. Okay?"

With her eyes fixated on Helena, Alex sits immediately and nods with an alluring smile.

Helena walks me to the lobby, and I burst into laughter. "Stop that, Laura."

"Goodness, that girl has it bad for you," I say

"Oh hush, you don't know that," Helena says sternly, then we both chuckle.

"What am I going to do with her if that's true, Laura?"

As I put my arm around her shoulder, I say, "Just think of what the old Laura would do—then do the opposite." I say with a playful wink and giggle.

Helena closes her eyes, opens them, and says, "My god, she was so gorgeous back then, but now—she's absolutely breathtaking."

Kissing my friend on the cheek, I look at her and say, "Helena, seriously. That woman in there is entirely smitten with you. She most likely has been all these years. Just go back and let this play out naturally. Okay?

Helena nods and says, "I'll call you in the morning."

As I walk away, I glance over my shoulder and say, "Or lunch." Then I wink and blow her a kiss, leaving Helena speechless for the first time in her life, most likely.

$$\approx$$

Jumping in my Alfa Romeo, I leave the parking lot, still grinning at that magical moment between Helena and Alex.

With the top down, I let my hair blow in the breeze as I drive to the airport to pick up the love of my life. As I wheel in, I spot her busy with her plane, so I just sit back with my shades on, grinning as I watch that perfect body of hers work to tie down the plane.

Glancing over her shoulder, she catches me watching and starts to laugh, knowing exactly what I'm up to. How I'm eyeing her unnerves her a little, but only enough to make her smile. She shakes her head, then walks toward me like she's still walking down a fashion runway. Whew, what a view!

How did I win the love of this sexy woman so long ago and still keep her interested? "Hi, gorgeous," she says as she hops beside me.

"You are the hottest woman on this planet, Erin Winslow," I exclaim.

She intertwines her fingers with mine and says, "Take me to the beach!" Grinning at me, she adds, "There are two blankets in the trunk, but stop so I can grab us some champagne."

Still smiling, I ask, "Why are there blankets in the trunk of my car?"

"Oh, you know, emergencies," she says with a playful wink. "And magical excursions."

Laughing, I shift my Sportster into gear and head east, feeling like a woman utterly, blissfully in love.

THANK YOU

Thank you for reading *Flying Miss Lomax*. I hope you enjoyed it!
I'd love it if you would take a moment to leave a review on Amazon and share your thoughts. Your feedback would mean so much to me!
Aven

Next up: *Romancing Miss Fitzgerald*. Helena finds herself captivated by Alex, the dark-eyed beauty who approached her table in the lobby of the Savannah Grand Hotel. Secretly in love with Helena for years, Alex now has a chance to reveal her feelings—though she harbors a dark secret. Don't miss this thrilling, passionate romance!

ALSO BY AVEN BLAIR

ABOUT THE AUTHOR

 Aven is a devoted author of age-gap sapphic lesbian romances, celebrated for her sweet yet fiery love stories that always promise a happily ever after. Writing from her quaint Southern town, she crafts captivating narratives centered around strong Southern women as they navigate love and life in historical settings. With a blend of warmth, humor, and emotional depth, Aven's stories enchant readers with unforgettable romances and her unwavering commitment to love in all its forms.